Ruby, Arizona

Joshua Owen

Second Edition Paperback

Cover Art designed by King Media, LLC

Joshua Owen
P.O. Box 903
Sheboygan, WI

ISBN: 9798622122583

Scripps O'Neill Publishing Company

Chapter One

The filthy trail evaporated from sight after the first mile, and the walls closed in as the canyon's summits slowly prevented all but indirect daylight.

The entire terrain was craggy, sparsely forested but with its own indigenous varieties of scrub brush: kidneywood, plumbago, red justicia, sage and several kinds called by different names by different people, and excepting early springtime the area for many miles in all directions was noticeably unlovely, although there were people who liked it for their own distinct reasons, and presumably there were people who would live nowhere else, and unquestionably it had its advantages although scenery, except in the total, overall sense, was probably not one of the reasons.

However, on a still early morning when a person could look in any direction and find nothing but rugged far-distant hazed mountains, and a cathedral-like ghostly magnificence as dawn arrived, it was possible to at least feel an empathy for whatever had created it, because in its own raw and uncompromising way, what it lacked in beauty it made up for in character.

Sheriff Lincoln Jameson summed it up well enough one time when he was bringing in a prisoner from Buckskin Canyon.

"Almost any other place I've been is prettier, but all pretty does is feed the soul, down here we got a land that feeds the needs of a lot of different folks-mostly outlaws."

But there would have been opposing opinions. Leslie West, the widow who operated a café opposite Jameson's jailhouse and deputy's office, and whose husband had ranched west of Fireside Spring, defended her part of the country not because her husband had given his life there making their living, but because she actually admired and appreciated it.

"This," she would say, "is a big land with no place in any corner of it for cowards," and if one limited one's outlook to that one essential, then perhaps it was not such a god-forsaken place after all. However, most people asked more of a homeland than that it require all its citizens to be brave. Some people just wanted a homeland to be handsome and grassy and forested and gentle, and safe.

The country hadn't been safe, ever. Now, there were hideous pits all through its grim and far-flung stony canyons. There were little bands , even, of wolf-like roaming fugitives and renegades and every stranger who entered Copper's General Store in Ruby, which was the only town throughout the territory, was either a lawman in search of a particular renegade, or a fugitive from such manhunting riders.

And yet Ruby actually had almost no serious breaches of the law. As for the outlying countryside-occasionally some leather-colored and provoked cowman would ride in from one of the distant ranches or some cow-camp and angrily denounce the whole blessed Territory of Arizona because he'd found a hide and part of a butchered carcass wearing his brand, and not a trace of a track where the thieves had gone after loading down their horses with his beef.

Lincoln Jameson rode out, never with a whole lot of excitement, to make an investigation. Lincoln was an accomplished tracker. He was also one of the best manhunters in the whole territory. But his private philosophy also included a conviction that it was a hell of a lot easier and cheaper to fed them than it was to make a lot of trouble for them and have them retaliate by raiding ranches, ambushing coaches, committing malicious murders at the unprotected, at least the unsuspecting, cow-camps scattered all over his area, and in general making life for the only deputy sheriff for several hundred miles, a living hell. Also, he knew for a fact his philosophy had undoubtedly kept him alive for the full ten years he'd been down there posted at Ruby. He'd actually been told that by the fugitives he occasionally went after.

It was a very fundamental case of elementary mathematics. There was one tough, skilled, rugged deputy sheriff. There were at least two hundred primeval miles, wild and as jagged as any land on earth, and there were at almost any given time dozens of holed-up outlaws, fugitives and renegades, stealthy trackers and manhunters, all of them staying far from the town and usually from the ranches as well, busy with their own affairs which were separate from local affairs, and all this being fact; where was the sense of that one deputy sheriff rushing forth like some greenhorn zealot to set the world right?

Lincoln Jameson was not an old man. He was barely into his thirties. He was compact and strong, with sunburnt light brown hair and dark green eyes. He had been a freighter, a free-graze cowman, a coach-driver, and one summer while awaiting full recovery from a set of broken ribs, the result of a bad fall on a running horse, he had tended bar, back in Nebraska.

Why he had arrived in Ruby was not as important as why he had remained there. He was a single man who, like anyone else, had very little to say about himself. No one had ever seriously thought he too was a fugitive, but neither had folks in general believed Lincoln Jameson had remained in Ruby because he was overwhelmed with the natural beauty of the forbidding countryside, or the town, which was ancient Indian in origin, comparatively recent Mex in architecture, and now almost wholly gringo in ownership and residency, and throughout all those deviations had remained thick-walled, unadorned, ugly and absolutely functional.

Deputy Jameson was one of those people who could readily adapt, and because he was not an individual who demanded a whole lot from life, who could get by adequately on very little in fact and be happy while doing it, he may have in fact liked Ruby and the surrounding countryside.

There was some reason to believe this. He one time told Leslie West that contentment and happiness were things a man carried inside himself and landscapes nor anything else had a hell of a lot to do with it.

It was a good point to make in a place where very few people ever tried to define the things in life which filled a person's days from morning until night, good, bad, or otherwise.

Murray Foster, who shod horses, repaired wagons and rigs, and rented out a few animals now and then in his combination smithy-liverybarn, put it succinctly by saying if people came to a country like this, they sure as hell were running from something, and if they stayed in a country like this, it just plain didn't take much to satisfy them.

Murray was a good example. He had shot a man to death in Omaha. He swore it was a fair fight. The authorities swore with equal vehemence that the dead man had not had a gun on him when he'd been killed-and that was plain murder.

Murray made no secret of his crime. Fifteen years later he was still swearing to high heaven that man had been carrying a gun.

After fifteen years there were probably very few people, even back in Omaha, who knew or cared. Lincoln Jameson was one of them, and once when a travelling peddler who had heard the Murray Foster legend at the cantina opposite the stage company's corral yard, had asked Lincoln why he had never done anything, the deputy sheriff answered very candidly that if Omaha had as crime-free a country as Lincoln had down in Ruby it would happen up there as it happened down here, because folks minded their own business.

That certainly was not the reply the peddler had expected, and it was not noticeably profound, but it reflected the attitude of Lincoln Jameson about a whole range of things, including nosy peddlers.

It was not inconsistent with the nature of the area nor of the town that people's pasts were their own concern, and providing whatever they might have been somewhere else, and which had got them into trouble, was not carried over into Jameson's territory, he was just like about everyone else, perfectly content to let sleeping dogs lie.

There were some crimes which were considered inexcusable by all cow-country standards. Fortunately they were very rarely committed, and even more rarely did the outlaw who committed them live to get as far towards the border country as Jameson's bailiwick. Otherwise, as Jameson had said, folks pretty much minded their own business. Those with pasts got one more chance to make it before heading on over the line into Mexico. Ruby was the last country town before the southerly border. If folks failed there, they had a straight shot overland down through the grueling desert and over the line into the dirty, dusty treacherous villages of Mexico.

It was a little like straddling a fence for Deputy Jameson. Everyone else in the territory from the distant cow-camps to Ruby, was saddled with the same problem, but only the law and those charged with enforcing it was in the forefront. Jameson's badge was also a target. Renegades of each variety arrived in the territory conditioned to avoid badges like the smallpox, and if that could not be managed, then they were conditioned to shoot on site.

Jameson was a born survivor. He was fast and deadly with a gun, but that was never enough in the border country or upon its fringes. It was also necessary to have vision from the back of one's head, to be able to scent-up trouble five miles before reaching it, and finally, it was also essential to be good at second-guessing people.

Chapter Two

Throughout the territory there were numerous hard-rock canyons with nearly perpendicular slick-stone walls. They were natural traps.

In less rocky areas vertical canyon walls could oftentimes be scaled by a man, if not necessarily a mounted man, because the walls were earthen and susceptible to the desperate carving of a cornered man. In this territory however, those canyon walls were almost always granite. If a fugitive allowed himself to be driven into those places he was cornered. That was all there was to it. He could not climb the sides nor the back barranca. He could throw down his weapons, curse a country as uncompromising, and raise both arms above his head.

Or he could fight it out. Those who had done that over the years were arranged in very neat rows out behind Ruby in the local cemetery.

There were stories of cornered renegades escaping. Some of those stories were in fact quite recent. Lincoln Jameson could attest without equivocation that in the past ten years not a single outlaw had escaped any posse he had led. Nor had an outlaw got off free when Jameson went out alone after one.

There were of course a great many renegades who were never caught, cornered in a box-canyon or any other way, because they had simply kept right on going, usually through the night, when they reached the territory. And there were also others who would lie over to rest their livestock for a few days, who knew how deadly the area was and did absolutely nothing to upset Sheriff Jameson.

Buckskin Canyon was the most notorious of those cul-de-sac-canyons. The reason for this was because the only approach to Buckskin Canyon was up through gently rolling country with trees and green grass clearly visible ahead.

Trees and greens meant water. In lower Arizona nothing was more to be desired particularly in spring and summer, than water.

Also, the delightfully enticing rolling territory with its trees and greenery up ahead, gradually worked its way up into one pair of land-swells roughly half a mile apart which paralleled one another, and which very mildly closed up until they were less than a quarter mile apart, and by that time they were also about thirty feet high with streaks of solid rock showing through where eons of rainfall had washed away the soil. One more mile and there was no dirt left on the sides as they closed in more, and also rose up higher and higher until they were particularly straight up and down. Then, the horseman was among those delightful trees and up to his animal's hocks in good grass-and he was also inside the most treacherous of all the box-canyons in the territory.

There was a spring back in there, plenty of stock feed, abundant shade, and if the rider happened to be a fugitive running ahead of Lincoln Jameson and a Ruby posse, he was as good as caught or killed.

There were four stone markers back in the canyon where some perfectly unsuspecting and well-intentioned wagoneers, a whole family of them, the father, mother, and two children, had been massacred in there unable to get out, by the band of stronghearted Apaches.

That had happened twenty-five years earlier. There had been no troublesome Indians around the territory in fifteen years, and that needless massacre had been in part responsible; the army had found the little children, had solemnly buried them under the stone markers besides their parents, then the army had without a word, gone after the Apaches. The army had not stopped until there was not a visible Apache left. The army had made such an impression that twenty-five years later the few Indians who still occasionally rode through, or made canyon-camp, were as discreet as ghosts.

There were range men who believed Buckskin Canyon was haunted. There were Mexicans living on the outskirts of town who would not go into Buckskin Canyon at the end of a lasso behind a ridden horse.

Of all those funnel canyons-called by the Mexicans *embudos*- none had as much history behind it and yet there was no sign, no written legends, not even any complete agreement among even the old timers about the past of Buckskin Canyon. In fact there were two stories about how it got its name. One legend had it that when the Confederates were making their desperate overland drive to reach California during the Civil War in order to confiscate that stored gold out there, they had stockpiled buckskins in the canyon.

Another story-this one may have been closer to the truth since it preceded the Civil War by at least half a century-had it that formidable Mexican Generalissimo Antonio Lopez de Santa Anna sent a battery of sword wielding Mexicans into the canyon to instill fear and respect in some Arizona rebels, and Buckskin Canyon was where they clashed. Outnumbered by hundreds, the Mexicans traded their buckskin trousers in exchange for liberty.

Lincoln Jameson preferred this Mexican legend to the other one. But he really was not very interested in local history or in any kind of history for that matter.

He appreciated Buckskin Canyon though. Over the years it, more than most of the other canyons he had also sought to use the same way, had helped him corner fugitives. Therefore when the stocky, dark and dusty rider entered Ruby with a Deputy U.S. Marshal's badge under the lapel of his coat, and handed Jameson the wanted dodger, worn and limp and sweat-stained, Jameson's first question was: "Has this son of a bitch ever been through the territory before, to your knowledge, Marshal? Because if he hasn't been, then maybe we stand a fair chance at catching him. Providing he isn't ahead of you and isn't riding on south."

The quiet expressionless federal manhunter answered curtly. "He ain't been through here before, Sheriff. He ain't been anywhere near this territory before. Read the dodger; he's fifty-eight years old, been in the federal prison up at Durango in Colorado for twenty of those years, and before that, he rode range in Montana and Wyoming. That didn't pay good enough so he robbed the bank at Shelton on the Wyoming-Montana line, and murdered the banker. For that he got life imprisonment, served twenty and escaped, and now he's down here somewhere."

"You trailed him down here, Marshal?"

"I trailed him to within ten miles of this town, Sheriff. And he didn't bypass me because he's riding a worn sorrel horse. I'll tell you something else about him—after twenty years of loafing in prison he just ain't tough enough for this sort of living."

Lincoln Jameson rolled a cigarette and lit it, blew smoke and skeptically eyed the Deputy U.S. Marshal. "You know how far it is from Durango, Colorado, to Ruby, Arizona Territory? Marshal, if he's made that ride without you catching him then he's tough."

The dark and expressionless federal lawman eyed Jameson as though he had no use for Cowtown deputy sheriffs. He arose, beat dust from his clothing with his hat before dropping it upon the back of his head, and said, "I got to go south to make contact down there and set up a blockage. I'll be gone maybe two, three days...By the way, my name's Buck Whitney. I'll look you up when I get back."

Jameson went to the door with the deputy marshal, saw him out, closed the door to keep the heat out and returned to his desk to study the dodger.

The fugitive was indeed fifty-eight years of age. It listed his date of birth on the dodger. His name was Chuck Hollister, he was a native of Montana and although the dodger spelled out his original crime and the fact that he had escaped, it did not say Hollister was dangerous, which may, or may not, have had some significance. In any case

Lincoln Jameson was under no delusion. There was no such thing, in his opinion, as an un-dangerous fugitive from the law.

He waited out the heat of the day, then went up to the corralyard to talk to the driver who had brought in the daily coach from around Springfield to the north.

The driver had seen no solitary horsemen anywhere along the way from the north, and at the stone trough mid-way where he was obligated by company regulations to halt and water stock, he had seen no sign at all of there having been anyone around at the trough ahead of him. He did, however, remember one thing. Someone roughly parallel to the coach about seven miles north of town and possibly a mile or a mile and a half west of the stage road, over in the broken, canyon-country, had signaled with a heliograph.

At least the driver, who had seen his share of heliograph signaling during his earlier years when army patrols had been all throughout the territory, thought it was a heliograph signal.

The reason he thought so was simple enough. There was no other way for a series of brilliant flashes of white-hot reflected sunlight to come and go like that unless they had been made by a reflector held in someone's hand.

"I'd guess he was maybe somewhere in the vicinity of Buckskin Canyon, Deputy. Maybe a little this side of it. I didn't see the signals until he was about finished or maybe I could have pinpointed them better. But he was not too far from Buckskin, I'd bet new money on that."

Jameson crossed to the cantina. It had been a hot day. Normally the real heat did not arrive for another month or two. But there were no guarantees about that either. In Arizona, there were an entire series of variables folks could not count upon, and the weather in springtime was one of them.

The barman was a newcomer to town, a pale man with fishy eyes, the kind that bulged and seemed unable to move very much. Jameson did not have to look at the barman if he chose not to. There were two large paintings over the barback, both of very voluptuous women, one woman was a few shades darker and heftier than the other one. No one knew now who had painted those portraits but whoever he had been he had provided something to take a man's mind off the heat, outlaws, anything else, and it could be done in accordance with the preferences of everyone. Some liked their women whiter and some liked their women darker.

Jameson had no particular preference in that area. He had never been married and now at his age he did not expect to ever be married. As for women in general, he liked to admire pretty ones the same as any other man, but he had misgivings about their demands and their requirements once a man married one of them.

Murray Foster entered the saloon, shuffled to the bar mopping off sweat with a red bandanna, and paused to stare at the new barman. Then he sighed and ordered beer, turned and wiped his neck as he said, "Lincoln, it's going to be another of those damned hot and dragged-out summers. You mark my word on it." The beer arrived and Murray handed over the five-cent piece to the fish-eyed barman and turned to watch the barman walk away. Then he drank half the beer and turned in the opposite direction to lean and say, "Where did he come from?"

Jameson shrugged. "I don't know. Maybe the stork brought him home like he brought you and me."

Foster drained his glass and beat the bottom of it atop the bar. Without looking around he relinquished his hold and as the barman took the glass away to be refilled Murray fished out his bandana again and wiped his face and neck.

"Had to go south and hunt for some strayed damn horses this morning," he announced. "Hot out there in that stone-canyon country."

Jameson was interested. "See anyone out there?"

"Three fellas with a horse-trading wagon. They had a camp set up at Buckskin Canyon, happy as clams. They knew where my strays had gone and all I had to do was follow the tracks they set me onto."

The refilled glass came back. Murray paused to down half of this one too before speaking again. "I got drier than a damned mummy out there."

"See anyone else?" the lawman asked. "A solitary rider somewhere maybe north or east of Buckskin Canyon?"

"Not another mortal soul," exclaimed Murray. "Tracks though, between town and the canyon, where some fella rode down and maybe had himself a look, then rode off to the south-west again. Are you looking for someone in particular, Lincoln?"

"Yeah, some older man, grey, riding a tired sorrel horse."

Foster drained his second glass. "Never saw him," he declared, and turned to go shuffling back out into the late afternoon heat, wiping his face and neck again.

It was cool in the saloon because the building was one of the few remaining structures of Mexican origin which had walls made of mud bricks and which were three feet thick for just this purpose; to keep heat out in summer and to keep it in during winter.

Jameson remained at the bar, the only customer until a pair of range men walked in beating off dust. One was a Mexican and the other one was just as dark but with taffy hair and light blue eyes.

Henry Cooper, the swarthy proprietor of the general store down the road a piece and on the same side as the saloon, arrived looking as glum as he usually looked.

He was still wearing his black cotton sleeve-protectors, but the apron had evidently been left back in the store. He angled over to stand near Jameson as he nodded for a beer, then clasped both hands atop the smooth old bar top and put a skeptical gaze upon Jameson.

"Are you expecting the James boys to rob the saloon this afternoon, Lincoln?"

Lincoln Jameson turned and put a grey stare upon the thicker and shorter man. "I was hoping they'd rob your store," he replied, and shoved his empty glass over when the fish-eyed barman arrived with Cooper's beer.

"I'll handle them if they do," retorted the dour-faced storekeeper, and picked up his glass to drink from it and to afterwards sigh with solid contentment as he put it aside. "That beer they make up at Springfield is almighty good, Deputy."

"If you've never drunk anything better," Jameson retorted, still annoyed by the storekeeper's earlier sarcasm.

The bull-like swarthy man leaned and finished his beer. "Sometimes this damned place makes me feel like I'm boxed in and can't get out."

Jameson said, "Why? You got the best business in the whole countryside. Why should you get sour?"

"How long have you been looking at the same faces around here, Lincoln? Ten years? Well, I have been doing it for something like twenty-five years."

"Take the stage up to Springfield for a few days" suggested the deputy sheriff.

"No thanks," grumbled the storekeeper. "If you care for another beer, I'll buy it. All right?"

"Naw," Lincoln said. "I don't want any more. I've got to take a little ride beyond the town and a stomach full of beer won't make it any easier."

"Where to?"

"Buckskin Canyon."

The storekeeper considered that for a moment before saying, "You're crazy. It'll be dark by the time you get out there. Even if you were looking for something it'd be too dark to see it."

Lincoln Jameson smiled, paid for his beer and walked out.

Chapter Three

The storekeeper was right, about an hour before Lincoln Jameson got close to the lower entrance to Buckskin Canyon the sun left, shadows started rolling in the way they can only do in a canyon-country, and because the moon was very new even when it ultimately arrived it gave off very little light. Coupled with the starshine, that moonlight was very sickly.

But Henry Cooper only knew part of what Jameson was up to. Cooper had said that Jameson would be unable to see whatever it was he might be looking for, out there, and that was definitely wrong. What Jameson knew about manhunting; Henry Cooper did not even suspect.

To find a fugitive in wild, up-ended rocky country like that area Jameson was quietly riding through the ghostly starshine, a knowledgeable manhunter did not look for the man.

Jameson crossed the mouth of the canyon, angled southward to a gravelly little pass he was familiar with, rode up it and down the far side of it, got beyond Buckskin Canyon then went northward along the sidehill of the western embankment until he located another game-trail and this time he allowed the bay horse to have its head, to pick its way up along the sidehill until, a little more than an hour later, when it was close to eight o'clock, the horse paused upon a wide rim and Lincoln Jameson climbed off, loosened the rope so the horse could pick bunch grass from the crevices as it dragged the reins, and Jameson went over to the nearby top-out above Buckskin Canyon and rolled a smoke which he lit behind his hat, then squatted on his heels and got comfortable.

He was not looking for the man. He was watching for the man's fire.

There was a fairly large cooking-fire below him and to his left, which was southward, down in among the big old raffish trees inside Buckskin Canyon.

That would be the horse-traders Murray had encountered. It was too much of a cooking-fire for a solitary rider in any case. But north and east a fair distance was the soft reflection of another supper fire and this was a small one. One man was over there. At the most, two men.

Jameson finished his smoke, guessing that the solitary man up yonder was not very far south from where the stage-driver had seen someone signaling with a mirror or a piece of polished steel.

Jameson went back to the horse, snugged up, mounted and turned back down off the slope. He knew the country to be traversed to reach the vicinity of that little cooking-fire as well as he knew the back of his hand. There were not very many springs nor waterholes in the country farther out, and those which existed were almost always at this time of the year being fully utilized by cowmen and their riders. Closer to Ruby there was more water and fewer people to use it. Even so, there was anything but an abundance, even right in the heart of town.

Somewhere to the north a few miles a wolf called and although he afterwards remained to listen and hopefully await a reply, there was no answer.

Closer, a horse nickered. Jameson unloaded at once, led his animal another hundred or so yards, left him behind a broken old Redstone spire tied to a stunted tree, and resumed his manhunt on foot.

The nickering horse had not alerted just Jameson. Somewhere up ahead was another man who was now also wide-awake and listening.

The night was bland and almost hot. It was as silent as a tomb after one of the forlorn wolf-call and the softer sound of the hobbled or tethered horse up ahead. It was in fact so quiet that eventually when he knew he had to cross clay gravel, Jameson removed both boots and went gingerly onward in his stocking-feet.

Even then an Indian might have been able to detect him. There was no such thing as a totally silent white-eyes, and for that matter there were extremely few totally silent redskins, but tonight all the stranger up yonder had to possess was normal hearing, which was why Jameson took almost an entire hour to cover something like two hundred and fifty yards.

Not because he wanted to take the stranger by surprise so much as he did not want the stranger to take *him* by surprise-with a bullet.

He saw the horse. A rib-bare, sore-backed, worn-out sorrel with a light mane and tail. The closer he got and the better sighting he had of that horse the less sympathetic he felt towards the desperately fleeing fugitive. There was no excuse for any person to treat an honest animal like that. Not even a desperate person.

He smelled tobacco smoke. It was pleasant. He guessed it came from a pipe, as he lifted out his Colt and eased ahead as far as a wind-smoothed tall reddish spire for harder-than-usual sandstone.

Upon the far side of this Redrock spire there was a scent of doused wood-coals, so evidently after the sorrel had nickered his owner had up-ended a canteen.

But the aroma of cooked food was still around there too. Jameson was hungry. All he'd had for supper was two glasses of beer and that hardly constituted a genuine substitute, even for drinking water, let alone food.

He paused in layers of night-gloom, made a careful study of all the rough and broken terrain upon the north side of the spire, and finally saw the man, nowhere near his camp, which was less than three hundred feet from Jameson dead ahead, but closer to Jameson's spire and to the east of it where he was just emerging from the rough far side of a continuation of the same hard sandstone out-thrust from which the redrock spire had been fashioned.

Jameson raised the gun a little, thumb-pad upon the hammer, and waited.

The stranger was a gaunt man, slightly stooped, with a soiled and stained grey Stetson shoved on the back of his head and silvery grey hair showing beneath it.

The man moved back in the direction of his camp. There was a blanket-roll over there, a booted carbine, a pair of big old army-style saddlebags, and a saddle. As the gaunt stranger got closer to his camp, he eased the sixgun into its hip-holster, which was all Jameson was waiting for.

The deputy sheriff called quietly and did not move out of his protective layers of night-gloom.

"Mister Hollister-don't touch the gun. Just stand right still and keep both of your hands out in front. That's fine. Now just hold it like that."

The fugitive's posture became even more stopped. Jameson understood that as he walked ahead a few yards until he found a decent rock ledge to sit on, then he sat and pulled his boots back on. Almost amiably he said, "Mister Hollister, is that sorrel of yours a mare?"

The reply was toneless. "Yes."

"Well sir, if you ever get another chance at your freedom let me recommend that you ride only geldings. They nicker quick enough, but a darned mare will do it quicker...Reach with your opposite hand now and shuck that belt-gun."

The fugitive obeyed, then turned to face Jameson without waiting to be told to. He squinted across the intervening little distance and said, "You're not Marshal Whitney."

Jameson stood up and stamped to settle both feet firmly then he said, "Nope. I'm from that town back yonder-Ruby. I'm the deputy sheriff stationed over there. Mister Whitney won't be back for a few days so I'll put you up at my jailhouse until he gets back."

Jameson studied the older man. Hollister was an ageing individual with rather handsome, even features and a thick mane of course grey hair. He did not look like someone who would rob a bank and deliberately shoot down a banker in cold blood, but then, maybe now he wouldn't; when he had been charged with doing that he had been about a quarter of a century younger.

Still, he was not the kind of fugitive Jameson was normally able to bring in. He was thirty years older than the other kind, and he did not look capable of the kind of treachery those other types were capable of.

Nonetheless Jameson said, "Sit on the ground. I got to tie your arms behind your back, and until I get your mare rigged out I got to belt you at the ankles too."

Hollister sat in the dirt, eyes looking anywhere but where Jameson was approaching. He refused to look at Jameson even while he was being tied, but afterwards when the deputy went over to sift through the camp for something to eat, Hollister said, "Are you really a lawman?"

Jameson looked up. "Where do you figure I got this badge?"

"You wouldn't be the first bounty-hunter to carry one of those in your pocket."

That was true enough. Jameson did not respond. He instead said, "If you haven't eaten your fill we got plenty of time. We don't have to be back down at Ruby before dawn."

Hollister put his sunk-set stare upon Jameson and in a scornful voice he said, "You're no deputy sheriff."

Jameson shrugged and sat down to eat. He was ravenous but did not realize it until he started filling up. When he was tapering off, he eyed the older man. "One question: When you got out of Durango, it would have been a lot closer for you to run up across Wyoming and Montana and get to Canada, than for you to come all the way down here and try to get into Mexico."

Hollister said, "You are wrong. That was the route they expected me to take. Shorter or not I'd never had been able to reach Canada." He made a mirthless smile. "Especially with Marshal Whitney on my back-trail. I'd never have survived our first meeting. I may not survive this one either, if you work for Whitney, but at least I came close. Didn't I?"

"Fairly close," conceded Jameson, and rose to his full height now that he was full. "Just set easy, Mister Hollister until I fetch in the horses. You can wallow all you'd like and I'll tell you one thing. No one has ever yet got free from my knots. You won't be able to do it either."

"You're a damned scalp-hunter, aren't you?" exclaimed the fugitive. "You're a crony of that murdering, back-shooting son of a bitch named Whitney!"

Jameson walked out of the camp to find and bring in their two horses and when he located the sorrel mare he felt even sorrier for her. She had evidently been a willing, faithful mount and in repayment she had been ridden almost to death.

When he got back where the slumped and disconsolate-looking fugitive still sat, he said, "I'd haul you in and lock you up if I never knew a damned thing about you, and you rode into town on this mare. Anyone who'd do this to any animal ought to be shot."

Hollister did not look up, did not give any clue that he had heard, and later, when Jameson went over to order him to stand up as soon as his ankles were freed, the fugitive just sat there until Jameson reached and hauled him up.

Even on the long ride out and around the northern high bluff which formed the northernmost barrier of Buckskin Canyon, Hollister was silent.

Jameson understood the man's depression. Hollister had come a very great distance under extreme hardship and stress, had come within only a few more days of reaching the border and safety over it down in Mexico, and had been checked up short north-west of Buckskin Canyon.

They had the lights of Ruby in sight when the fugitive gravely looked down there, then turned and said, "It's a handsome and pleasant town, bounty-hunter."

Jameson was smoking so he first removed the cigarette before he said, "You are as wrong as all hell on both counts. I'm not after you for any bounty, and that town up there is ugly as sin."

They were on the outskirts when Hollister spoke again. "Maybe I was wrong figuring you to be a bounty-hunter, but it really is a pleasant little old adobe town. It's got trees and water."

"And dusty roads, ugly stores, hot drinking water, and…" Jameson turned, looked at the older man besides him and let it end right there. It dawned on him to someone who had been looking at nothing but the inside of concrete and stone walls for twenty years, Ruby did look wonderful.

They tied up out front of the jailhouse. The nearest lighted building was the cantina across the road and northward. Otherwise, there was a sputtering carriage lantern alight out front of Murray's barn.

Jameson took his prisoner inside, lighted a lamp in the cell-room, locked Hollister in a clean cell, said, "I got to look after the horses," and left.

Murray Foster had an annoying habit of making a clucking sound when something bothered him. He looked at the sorrel mare and clucked. Jameson ignored the sound and handed over the mare's reins. "Grain her a little, give her a clean stall with fresh water and good hay."

Murray looked angry. "I know what to give her. I don't need anyone to tell me how to take care of horses-thank you!"

Jameson left his own animal down there also and as he turned back in the direction of the jailhouse and looked up the roadway, he saw that stage-driver he had spoken with earlier stalking across from the corralyard towards the cantina. It was that time of night. In fact, it was almost late enough now for some of the steadies in there to be calling it a night.

On an impulse he went over there, barged through the noisy throng of townsmen and rangemen, got a bucket of suds from the bar and took it back across to the jailhouse with him.

He did not let the prisoner out, he let himself into the cell. Jameson handed the beer to Hollister to take the first drink while Jameson built and lit a smoke, then he accepted the bucket back and also drank. He said, "A man is entitled to a couple of glasses of beer after a long day, Mister Hollister. You agree?"

The older man nodded and remained silent.

Jameson offered his makings. Hollister made no attempt to take the sack of tobacco or the papers. He looked over them at the deputy. "What do you expect me to be able to tell you?" he asked. "First beer, then a pleasant little conversation, and now the offer of a smoke. Deputy, you're wasting your time. I'm wanted for escape up in Colorado and that's all there is to it...I don't have any buried gold."

Jameson drew back the hand and gazed dispassionately at his prisoner. "You don't trust anyone, do you?"

"It hasn't done me a hell of a lot of good, Deputy."

"How do you know; when was the last time you tried it? Mister Hollister I only wanted to catch you. That's all. Otherwise I don't have any feelings about you one way or another. As for you figuring I'm trying to soften you up so you'll tell me where you've got a cache of gold or something," Jameson looked wry as he shook his head. "I've been hearing about those caches all my life and I've yet to see a single one."

He arose. The bucket of beer was still half full. He left the cell, locked it from the corridor and glanced back just once. Hollister was eyeing him with a faint, baffled look. Jameson turned and walked back to his office, closed and barred the cell-room door, flung aside his hat and went to the desk to sit down and write out for his records all he knew about his prisoner.

Chapter Four

The door opened quietly from out front. Jameson looked up without much interest expecting it to be someone from the cantina with a complaint about a drunk, and instead a lithe, leggy individual wearing faded work-trousers and shirt, along with a grey hat, stepped in, closed the door and turned towards Jameson with a cocked sixgun swinging up to bear.

He turned to stone. It was a girl. She said, "Put your gun atop the desk."

Lincoln obeyed, relaxed a little at a time studying her, and when she gestured towards the cell-room door he arose without waiting to receive the order. She halted him with a question.

"How many prisoners do you have in there?"

"One," he replied. "An older man."

"No others?"

"No ma'am. Not until I bring you back and lock you in there too."

She ignored that to say, "All right. Open the door, go down to Mister Hollister's cell and let him out. Deputy, don't think for one moment that I won't shoot you."

He stared steadily at her and groaned. He had done a dumb damned thing. He had forgotten what the coach-driver had said about Hollister signaling someone, but he had not considered it as seriously as he should have, and this was the result of that oversight-the girl with the gun in her fist.

"Who are you?" he asked.

She waggled the gun barrel. "Just open the door and don't do anything foolish."

She had the initiative. He turned, lifted down the door-bar and entered the gloomily lighted cell. Hollister was sitting on his bunk smoking a pipe. He looked around, leaned to look harder, then got to his feet and stepped to the front of the cell, eyes wide.

"Nellie!"

The girl spared him a glance. "Get your hat, we'll be on our way in a few minutes. Dad, lock the deputy in."

Hollister came out as Jameson swung the door open. He motioned for the deputy to enter the cell, then he closed the door and leaned to lock it. Jameson was looking at the girl. If Hollister had been in prison twenty years or so, then the girl, his daughter, must have been very tiny when he'd gone away because she did not look to be at the very most, twenty-one or twenty-two years old, and in fact Jameson would have thought her closer to eighteen. He said, "Nellie, just because I don't want to see you get shot, I'm going to give you a warning. If you go south for the border, you're going to ride into a waylaying bunch of posse men. Marshal Whitney went down there to arrange that border blockage."

She did not even glance at Jameson. She waited until her father had the cell locked, then she leathered that Colt pistol and turned to march back up to the front office with her father following.

Jameson removed his hat, tossed it upon the bunk, leaned to listen and when he heard the big old oak roadside door open and close, he went to a stool to sit down and tug off his boots. He was tired and although he had a room at the boarding house over on the street behind the main road to the east, tonight he was not going to be able to get over there so he got ready to sleep right where he was.

Providence in the form of Leslie West from the café across the road arrived, and when he called on her from the cell she came down there, stood with her hands on her hips to stare in at him, and when he told her where the keys were she went after them in silence-then it must have hit her up in the office, because suddenly she burst out laughing.

He was a little red in the face while he waited for her to release him. She struggled to keep her amusement from showing, but without total success, so when he went back up front, he ignored her while he got back his sixgun and put on his hat. Then he said, "Thanks. Now you got something to tell everyone who shows up at the café for breakfast."

Leslie West was two years older than Jameson. She had her sunburnt blonde hair cut short and close to her head. She was a shade taller than average for a woman, and she as solidly put together. She had direct blue eyes which could melt stone, or which could freeze an offensive cowboy to the bone.

She looked at Jameson with her direct look and said, "I'm not going to tell anyone, Lincoln. As I was closing a while ago a very attractive young girl came in for some coffee and asked if there was more than one law officer in town. That's all; and that's what I came over here to tell you because it seemed odd to me that such a pretty young thing...."

"That pretty young thing is the person who released a prisoner on me and locked me in that lousy cell, so you can save your sympathy." He looked around. "Blow out the lamp when you leave and snap the front door lock from the outside." He took down a booted carbine from the wall rack and left the office, taking long steps.

Without more than a hunch that they had continued southward towards the Mexican line he hastened to Murray Foster's place and had to rout Murray from his cot in the harness room. He had been hoping that Murray might have been awake, might in fact have rented a couple of his horses to the fugitives, and watched what direction they rode off in. Instead, a couple of minutes after he had shaken Murray awake the horse-trader went down his row of stalls and let out a squawk because two of his best horses were missing, and now Jameson had no way of actually knowing which way the horse thieves had gone.

He was annoyed so he got his own horse and rigged it out. He had in mind riding southward, but on a sashaying course which would enable him to ride back and forth, east and west, just in case he might be able to hear riders in some other direction. There was nowhere nearly enough starlight to read tracks by, so he was going to have to do this by ear-which was almost never successful-but anything beat sitting in the jailhouse under Leslie West's giggly stare.

Murray followed Jameson out front bitterly complaining about 'someone' being responsible for people like these horse thieves being loose to rob honest hard-working folks. He wanted to sign a complaint and Jameson told him he could sign a dozen of them, when Jameson got back, but right now Jameson was going to try and find these people.

He left town in an easy lope and followed the stage road for two miles, halting occasionally in the hope that either her or his horse might pick up a sound. A band of yapping coyotes on the move crossed from west to east and when they detected the man scent of Jameson they scattered among the backbrush on the east side of the road and deliberately bedeviled the man by seeming to be in a dozen places at the same time, a favorite pastime of coyotes.

Otherwise, Jameson did not pick up a sound.

He left the road riding westward. He kept on that paralleling course to the Mex border for three miles, then turned around and made his long sashay back towards the east. He covered about twice as much ground as he might have had to cover if this had been broad daylight when dust would have offered a tell-tale indication of the course of his outlaws, and despite all the time lost and territory traversed he failed to pick up a single significant sound, so just short of dawn he dismounted to rest his horse's back, and walking along leading the animal.

He had come to a broken field of horse-high rocks and paused there to roll smoke. Around him there was an immense sea of silence.

He was not going to find them. Not tonight, and in any case, even if he found their tracks after sunrise, they would be at least six hours ahead which meant he would not be able to overtake them in daylight either.

Losing outlaws was something lawmen never became accustomed to. Especially lawmen with pride in their craftmanship like Lincoln Jameson had.

He finally turned back towards Ruby, riding through a magnificent dawn as cool and refreshing as a man could hope a dawn might be. When he had the town in sight, he saw the dust rising northward where the morning stage had departed earlier and was now dusting it northward out of Ruby. He cursed about that too, but when he finally got back and left his horse with Murray to be cared for and walked purposefully up to the corralyard, he was rewarded with something to mitigate his earlier gloom. He had been afraid the driver of the morning stage might be the driver he wanted to talk to. It wasn't. The man he sought was on his was to Leslie West's café and Jameson caught up with him midway along.

The driver greeted him quietly, looking suspiciously at the lawman's rumpled clothing. "You look like a man that's been up all night," he asserted, and Jameson mechanically smiled.

"Yesterday, when you saw those heliograph signals from west of the coach-roach," he said, refreshing the driver's memory, "did you have any passengers aboard your stage?"

The driver nodded. "One, a young girl."

Jameson sighed. "Thanks," he said and turned on his heel leaving the driver to lift his hat, scratch, and waggle his head a little before resuming his way towards Leslie West's place.

Jameson went to the boarding house to shave and scrub and to put on some clean clothes. He had now figured out how Hollister and the girl-his daughter-had made their contact. What he did not know at this point was why, if she had been with her father last night when Jameson caught him, she hadn't thrown down on Jameson, either at the camp north of Buckskin Canyon, or perhaps along the trail as he was herding her father along towards town.

He left his room heading for the café and breakfast, convinced that the girl had most certainly had her own reason for waiting to throw down until her father and his captor were both at the jailhouse.

Anyways, that was not very important. Not at this point, anyway. What he had to devise now was how he was going to get those two back. He was obviously not going to be able to run them down. Whichever route they took out of town was for the time being known only to them. But Jameson was a very patient, very steadily persevering, and very stubborn individual. When he entered the café and found the place empty, he nodded at Leslie and sat down at the counter with a steady look up in her direction. She was a very good-looking woman, even to a man who hadn't slept last night and who hadn't had a decent meal in even longer. But when she came over he said, "By golly, you know what, Leslie? I do declare you're putting on weight."

She leaned down and smiled directly into his face. "Someday I'm going to kill you," she said in her sweetest tone of voice. "Or maybe I'll just tell folks how I had to release our heroic deputy sheriff from his own jail cell where a little slip of a fifteen or sixteen-year-old girl locked him in."

"She's at least twenty-one and maybe twenty-two or three...What do you have for breakfast this morning?"

"Don't change the subject! You rode all night-and?"

"I can't see in the dark."

"In other words you rode the duff off your horse for nothing."

"Leslie, just get my damn breakfast, will you?"

She kept smiling at him and leaning down. She was a beautiful sturdy woman and when she leaned, she also managed to abundantly fill her cotton blouse. "Lincoln, that prisoner she turned loose...."

"Her father," Lincoln corrected. "Escaped from Durango up in..."

"An old man and a slip of a girl," Leslie West murmured, and straightened back to turn and head for the kitchen, which was separated from the counter by a floor-length curtain covered with some highly improbable blue flowers larger than cabbages. From out there as she prepared breakfast she said, "They'll make it over the line."

He thought so too.

"And Mex border towns are no place at all for a pretty little girl. They are full of the scum of both nations."

He rolled a smoke in silence and lit it.

She sniffed tobacco smoke, dried her hands and took him out a cup of fresh coffee. "Get her out of there, Lincoln," she said quietly. "The men down there are worse than animals."

He raised the cup as he said, "A deputy U.S. marshal has a trap down along the border for the man. He won't know there's a girl along with the old man." He suddenly remembered how easily she had got the drop on him. He also remembered what Marshal Buck Whitney looked like, so he doubted very much that the girl would be able to do that again. And Whitney would not be alone, the way Jameson had been.

"Lincoln, where does it say federal peace officers can't be just as bad with young girls as outlaws? Go down there and bring her out."

He tasted the coffee. It was fresh. No one could make coffee the way Leslie West could make it. He set the cup aside and wrinkled his nose. "My breakfast is burning." He said, and Leslie fled. She could move like greased lightening when she had to.

He had never heard her swear and he was not positive he heard her do it now, but it sounded suspiciously like someone beyond that curtain with the huge blue flowers on it said, "Damn it!"

Jameson had not considered the plight of the girl named Nellie Hollister once she and her father got over the line; *if* they got over the line.

He had not particularly cared for Marshal Whitney, but that had been a snap judgement; Whitney had not remained in town long enough for Jameson to get to know him. As for Whitney bothering Nellie as Leslie had implied, Jameson was too good a judge of men to believe that would happen. Whitney was a manhunter and that was all he was; successful manhunters had no time for girls, nor even for big armloads of women like Leslie West. Jameson was prepared to bet new money on it.

But those men over the line in the dirty and depraved Mexican villages south of the border were something different.

Before entering the café, he had only been concerned with catching them and fetching them back to his jailhouse. Now, thanks to Leslie West, something else was beginning to bother him a little.

Chapter Five

He did not believe Hollister was going to make it over the line, and if the girl had listened at all when Jameson had warned her, he was half of the opinion that she would not let her father continue on down there.

But that was pure guesswork. Hollister had been thinking in terms of crossing the border for a long time, since he fled from Colorado. Would he be willing to change his mind now?

Jameson did not know Hollister either, except to say that he was a man of very little trust and probably the same amount of faith.

At the jailhouse Jameson was sweeping out when one of the corralyard-hostlers came over with his mail and departed. The stage company which had the mail-hauling franchise from the government, also happened to have the town franchise, so all mail passed through the hands of the company manager for Ruby, a burly, bearded man named Pete Clifford.

Jameson already had two wooden crates full of wanted posters and this morning he got three more to add to his collection. None of the three received in the morning's mail were about Chuck Hollister, not that Jameson was at all surprised. In his experience those flyers only arrived after the outlaw had passed through.

He chucked the three dodgers into his file crates, finished cleaning the jailhouse and was about to go down to see if the sorrel mare was responding to decent humane care for a change, when a thick, bull-necked unsmiling dark individual rode up the roadway from the south of town.

Deputy U.S. Marshal Buck Whitney.

Jameson stood in the shade out front of his office and stared. He would have bet money Whitney was down along the border like a cat waiting for the canary.

The federal officer turned in at the jailhouse tie rack, clasped both hands over the saddle horn and stonily gazed at deputy Jameson. "You had him, and he got away," Whitney stated, and leaned to kick loose a foot and swing to the ground. He tied the horse and leaned upon the rack. "Just how did that happen, Deputy?"

"Easy as falling off a chair," stated Jameson, irritated by the man's tone and by his look. "And since you knew all about your fugitive why didn't you tell me there were two of them?"

Whitney said, "There weren't two of them."

"Try again, Marshal. There was Chuck Hollister and Nellie Hollister. I brought them in, and she came along nice as you please and threw down on me."

Whitney frowned. "His daughter?"

"Yeah. Didn't you know he had one?"

"Of course I knew. There is nothing about them I don't make it my business to know before I take after them. Only his daughter Nellie is a schoolteacher up in Tie Siding, just over the line above Colorado into Wyoming."

Jameson said, "Maybe that's where she is supposed to be, but right now she's riding a stolen horse besides her father."

"What direction?"

"If I knew that, Marshal, I'd be out there."

"Would you for a fact," muttered the federal officer and turned to unloop his reigns and lead the horse down to Murray's barn.

Jameson walked with him. "Why aren't you down with your posse or whatever it is, along the border?"

"I told you, Deputy, I was going down there to set it up. I never said I aimed to camp down there with them. Part of my scheme was to ride back up here where maybe Hollister would have seen me on the road and feel so safe he'd bust out into a run for the border, right into the hands of my friends the *Rurales*."

Jameson stopped dead still. *"Rurales*? I thought you said you were going down there to…"

"Establish a blockade, Deputy, and that's exactly what I did. I offered to split the Colorado reward with the *Rurales*, the Mexican constabulary police…"

"You don't have to explain to me about the Mex *Rurales*, Marshal. I've had more than my share of dealings with those murderous, treacherous, blood-thirsty bastards." Jameson remembered something and said, "Whitney, those bastards will kill him on sight. They'd kill a law-abiding gringo on sight, let alone a wanted man. You knew that, didn't you?"

The stocky, bronzed and dark-eyed federal deputy turned, and they exchanged hostile looks. "Deputy. I know your territory and I know your personal reputation. That's why I chose to run this go-round myself and cut you out of it. Hollister is a fugitive, a wanted man, an outlaw. He was lucky they didn't hang him quarter century back. Since then he's had twenty safe years with taxpayers feeding and clothing him and paying for the roof over his head. And now he chose to break away and make a sporting run for it…"

"Which makes him your clay pigeon."

"Yes. If you want to put it that way, Deputy, that is exactly what it makes him. But I certainly never figured on the girl being with him. Can you be positive?"

"Go ask the stage-driver who brought her into Ruby on his southward run," replied Jameson. "And there is something else I'm going to tell you, Marshal. If those

Rurale partners of yours kill Hollister I'm going to write the government, the governor in Colorado, and anyone else I can think of like maybe the Attorney General of the U.S. and tell them you are a goddamn butcher."

Jameson stepped ahead and strode angrily in the direction of Murray Foster's barn. Down there, he paused long enough to drink from a hanging bucket and when Murray came out to squint, Jameson said, "What the hell do you want-two-bits because I drank some of your water?"

Murray blinked. "No, not at all. Drink as much as you like. I never charged a man for a drink of water in my life…say, what's eating at you? Listen, Deputy, I'm not saying a single thing about you hanging around town when horse thieves done raided me last night."

Jameson entered the barn, hunted up the stall of the sorrel mare, saw that although she still looked battered and ridden down, her eyes were bright again and someone had greased all her bruises and nicked places, and while he leaned there looking in, the mare went back to her manger to chew hay.

At noon he returned to Leslie's café without really thinking. It was something he had been doing for years, walking in over there for his meals. It did not occur to him until he was inside and saw the look on her face that he had blundered. She was very clearly still thinking of that pretty slip of a girl.

It was too late to turn and depart. Leslie motioned for him to take a place up at the north end of the corner which was closest to her cooking area, and the moment he reluctantly dropped down and removed his hat, she said,

"She fooled you, didn't she? Instead of heading south for the border she and her paw went north into the foothills where there is less rocks and more grass."

Jameson stared. "Who told you that?"

"Couple of range riders who were here about an hour ago. They saw an older man, grey as a badger, and a slip of a girl riding with him, heading northward over on the west range. Out about three miles they said." She stepped to a counter to get a piece of crab apple pie for him, and as she leaned to put it down, she said, "I'm so glad for her. It worried me sick thinking of her being down in Mexico, as pretty as she is and all. Just sit still now and I'll fetch you..."

"North and west towards the foothills?"

"Yes. I just told you that Lincoln."

"Give me the descriptions exactly as those range men gave them to you, Leslie."

"Lincoln, I just did that." She then proceeded to repeat what she had said a moment earlier. He cut her short with a hand gesture. "Get me a bowl of chili or something that will stick to a man's ribs. Now I got more riding to do. How far out did these cowboys see Hollister and the girl?"

"Eight or ten miles. Lincoln, you can't overtake them. Not unless you sprout wings."

He said, "Don't you have a bowl of chili, Leslie?"

She had one and she departed to get it. The moment her back was turned he arose, grabbed his hat and bolted out of there. He went over to the corral yard and looked up disagreeable and bearded Pete Clifford to ask when the next northbound coach was leaving town.

Clifford pointed to a thick, stubby arm. "That one be leaving in maybe fifteen minutes. Why?"

"I want a seat on it."

Pete Clifford put his dark stare upon Deputy Jameson. "All right. It's all right with me, Lincoln."

They completed the transaction then and there. Afterwards the lawman loped down to the jailhouse office, got another booted Winchester from the wall rack, scuttled over to the general store to fill a small flour sack with tinned food, and hastened back to the corral yard ready to travel.

Pete Clifford came forth from his office carrying some manifests for fast light freight. He was handing the papers to his driver when he saw Deputy Jameson with the flour sack and the booted carbine. He turned to say, "What's going on?"

Instead of answering Jameson climbed into the coach; breaking a company rule about passengers not getting in until the coach was out front parked before the office. The gun guard walked up looking displeased. He leaned in, saw the badge, saw the man wearing it and turned away.

Not even Pete Clifford who was invariably disagreeable if a company edict was violated, said anything, and when the driver came along pulling on gauntlets as he walked along, he no more than glanced in, then swarmed up the side of his coach to the high seat, sand out to the four-horse-hitch, turned the clumsy string animals and wheeled equipment with awesome expertise and walked his coach out through the log gateway where a swamper holding a lard bucket of axle-grease waved that the roadway was clear. The driver cut it wide. Unnecessarily wide in fact but a little grandstanding to let the town know how good he was, never went unappreciated. When his leaders just barely scuffed the yonder plank walk with their shoes, then kept swinging until they were lined out northward, several of the elderly spit-and-whittle club nudged one another and chuckled. They at least appreciated how deftly that driver could handle his hook-up.

Jameson composed himself. He was a very unique individual. He could actually sleep on a pitching, swaying stagecoach.

He knew just about every trick there was to this manhunting business. The foremost trick was not to wear yourself put. That is when mistakes are made, sometime deadly mistakes. He braced himself, put his hat aside and slept. He was the only passenger, and that made it possible for him to hoist both feet to the opposite seat to set himself so that the pitching and swaying would not spill him into the lower area between the seats.

The other aspect of this manhunt which he was employing was the part Leslie West had seemed to derive so much pleasure from. Leslie had said that slip of a girl had fooled Jameson and that he could not catch her now. That was an error. Jameson was embarked upon a scheme to prove how wrong Leslie had been, and it was really very elemental. Four horses in harness ahead of a light mud-wagon stagecoach could gallop all day, and a saddlehorse could not. That was how knowledgeable manhunters closed distances and arrived at their destination so much fresher than their prey that no one could make a fair comparison.

He slept all the way up the north roadway even after they reached the wash-boardy stretch of road just south of the foothills where runnels of run-off rainwater kept the road badly ridged and rutted. He slept beyond that for a mile up into the foothills, then he awakened when his head hit the roof as they dropped into a chuckhole and waddled up out of it on the far side.

He swore, groped for his hat, crushed it atop his head and risked another bump by leaning to poke his head out to look around.

He knew exactly where they were. He had ridden these foothills so many times, and the high mountains farther along, that he could tell within a couple of miles where anyone on horseback would be, providing he knew where they had started from and also providing he had some idea of how urgent their ride was.

There were long shadows coming in from the west, slanting along the upper reaches of the far mountains from west to east. Farther up the sun was still brightly shining. It would continue to light the great peaks until the very last vestige of daylight was ready to depart.

Between the foothills and the higher mountains which were actually many miles distant although because the air was as clear as crystal they looked closer, there was a miles-deep up-ended rocky country with pockets of trees and grassy little wide canyons. It was ideal country for people with livestock because, unlike the territory back down around Ruby, it had abundant feed. The people Deputy Jameson was looking for were in that intermediate country somewhere. He was certain of it, unless the information Leslie had provided him with was incorrect start to finish.

He picked a spot he thought would be at least a couple miles north of where the Hollisters would be riding, let the coach carry him all the way up the slope to the spot which would roughly parallel the area he figured they had to be in, and when the driver was allowing his hitch to settle down into a slow, pulling walk, Jameson beat on the side of the coach with his fists until the gun guard leaned and looked downward with a disgusted expression on his face.

"What's all wrong with you, Deputy?" he said.

"Half mile up ahead where there is a stand of junipers, let me out," called back Jameson, and the gun guard straightened up to reply this message. The driver looked ahead, looked on both sides, spat amber chewing tobacco and shrugged his mighty shoulders. It was all right with him. The less weight he had to burden his hitch with going over the long-spending pass, the better he liked it.

"Probably got a still up in here somewhere," muttered the driver, and got ready to set the wheel brake. "Darn fool would have to pick a place that ain't flat and the horses will have to hold all the weight."

That was indeed what happened. The driver set his brake but the horses still had to lean into their collars to keep the coach still until Jameson climbed out with his carbine and his flour sack of provisions, and waved the stage onward.

The driver was a seasoned hand; the coach hardly rolled backwards a quarter turn of the larger rear wheels before the horses picked up the slack and hauled their chain-tugs taut as they moved ahead without a single lunge or jerk.

Jameson walked to the underbrush and trees on the west side of the road. Within five minutes there was no sign of him out though there, but southward only about a mile where the trees were fewer and the grass was taller and thicker, he could not cover a hundred yards without being seen by anyone up this rugged, variegated rolling and mountainous territory who happened to be looking.

There was game-sign and a little cattle and horse sign, but he went higher and deeper into the forest he lost all track of domestic livestock and came across only the marks of wild animals.

Range horses and cattle knew by instinct not to go up into the higher forested country which was the home of catamounts and bears-and quite often two-legged fugitives in need of beef to eat and fresh horses to ride.

Chapter Six

Jameson stopped at the little tree-shaded spring he had headed for after leaving the stage road. There were young pines and some scattered oak trees up there but most important, there was an unimpaired southward view from that place, as well as an excellent view to the east and west.

He drank spring water, tossed his hat aside in the grass, pulled up the flour sack and dug out a can of sardines and also a can of apricots. He ate slowly and placidly while keeping a steady watch for movement southward and on both sides. Once, he saw a cinnamon bear and another time he saw a shaggy old rough-looking lonely wolf, probably the last of his breed in the Arizona hills. But there was no sign of riders, and by the time Jameson had finished his meal he was beginning to have the first misgivings. He probably should have asked Leslie more about those range men who had informed her of having sighted the Hollisters, or someone who looked like them.

On the other hand, he had hours yet. The difficulty was that when a man was uncertain of something, waiting only heightened it.

Jameson made a smoke, leaned back against a tree and became watchful and as motionless as an Indian.

What he eventually saw, and not too distant either, was a clan of coyotes come running out of a deep arroyo, scattering in all directions once they reached the upper land. Anyone who knew much about game animals knew coyotes did not behave like that without a very good reason.

Jameson stubbed out his cigarette and waited. Five minutes later a rider also came up out of that arroyo, and behind the first rider there emerged a second one.

Jameson expelled a long, relieved, breath. That foremost rider was about the size of a fifteen-year-old boy. The second rider was larger, older and a little stooped. The distance was too great for a more detailed sighting, but Jameson was satisfied.

He sat and watched, surmised the course they would follow in their onward ride towards the more forested northward country up where he was sitting, and sighed, arose with the carbine and started moving westerly, but on an angle which took him up the slope a little more and deeper into the trees. He guessed he had about a mile to travel before he was near enough to where the Hollisters would come up there for the interception, but he was wrong because Nellie Hollister turned slightly to the east, to avoid some upthrusts, and that put her even closer. By the time Jameson could guess about where he would stop them, they were coming almost directly at him.

There were only a few scattered trees where they were riding now. Jameson did not want them to be in among the denser stands of timber because while he did not expect a lot of difficulty, he preferred not to invite it nor risk it, either.

Finally, from his point of vantage beside a tree where welcome shade covered everything for a hundred feet in all directions, he could not make out the details. He had no doubt the identity of those riders since his first sighting of them, but now they were close enough for him to confirm it. Old Hollister seemed more tired than ever. He probably had a right to feel that way. Twenty years in prison hadn't injured very many people to the rigorous hardships of range-country existence on the outside, and someone who hadn't ridden a horse in that length of time was bound to be suffering a little.

Jameson raised the carbine, checked it, left the hammer flat down and when he thought they were within range, he held the gun aimed in their direction with a thumb upon the hammer. He did not want to shoot anyone, least of all the girl and an older tired man.

The girl stopped once in shade and sat looking back. Jameson distinctly heard her say, "Dad? Another mile and we'll be far enough into the trees to rest for the balance of the day. Look back there; no sign of anyone tracking us."

Chuck Hollister did not look back. He smiled at his daughter and motioned for her to head on up-country again. She obeyed, riding directly towards Jameson's tree.

He looked from the riders to the horses. They were string, sleek animals. No wonder Murray had had such a fit.

Another dozen yards and the girl's horse humped up to climb a little. After he settled flat on his feet again Jameson moved a little to one side of his shielding tree and the girl did not see him at once but her horse did, and his reaction was to suddenly falter his stride, and that alerted the rider.

The girl saw Jameson and the pointed Winchester when she was less than fifteen yards from him. She did not react with the abrupt astonishment Jameson had expected. She instead drew reign, halted her beast, settled both hands atop the saddlehorse and sat gazing at him until her father eased up beside her-and also saw the deputy sheriff with the pointed carbine.

Chuck Hollister recognized Jameson. His daughter no doubt also did but it was the older man who said, "I don't believe it. I don't believe you could get up here ahead of us."

Neither of them looked nor acted the least bit dangerous. Jameson was inclined to give them that benefit of the doubt, too, except that they had once before fooled him. "Empty the holster," he told Hollister. He looked at Nellie after her father had dropped his weapon to the ground. "You too, miss."

She was not wearing a hip-holster, she had a shoulder-holster under the jacket she had on and when she lifted out the weapon it was not the same big single-action Colt she had got the drop on Jameson before with, it was a Colt Lightning sixshooter, much smaller and lighter, and double rather than single, action.

"Breaking out of prison is bad enough but stealing those two horses is a lot worse in my eyes, folks. Dismount and stay up front where I can see the pair of you-and Mister Hollister, you know the rest of it. Sit down so I can bind your arms behind you."

They obeyed. Hollister was as taciturn as he had become that other time. He was more tired now, though, than demoralized. As least that was Jameson's guess.

The girl did not act fierce nor especially defiant and while Jameson was trussing her arms behind using her own belt, she said, "I don't usually misjudge people the way I misjudged you, Mister Jameson."

He smiled. "That'll work both ways, young lady. I owed you this for what you did to me."

"Who let you out?" she asked.

"The lady who runs the café where you ate and asked how many lawmen there were in town."

The girl looked up. "Of course. That was foolish of me. I should have guessed you and she would be good friends. You are both single."

That intrigued Jameson. "How did you know that?"

"The storekeeper told me. I talked to several people once I got to town, Mister Jameson. That was part of my scheme."

He settled back looking down at her. "How did you know I was brining your father in?"

"Saw you," she answered succinctly, and did not elaborate on that.

"Why did you wait until I had him locked up to jump me?"

"I had to, Mister Jameson. While you were bringing him in, he was so close that the first sign of trouble you would have shot him first. At the jailhouse, you put him in a cell, then went back to your office."

Jameson continued to squat there regarding the handsome, slight, leggy young woman. Then, as he eventually moved to arise, he said, "Shoot hell. I wasn't going to shoot anyone. Your pappy or anyone else. He wasn't my headache anyway; he was that federal marshals headache."

Jameson went over to her father and the older man said, "You wouldn't have anything to eat by any chance?"

"Back where I watched you, near a little spring, and as soon as you're both tied," he answered, "we'll head over there."

Jameson was conscious of the girl watching everything he did. When he was tying her father's arm he suddenly looked up. The girl's glance fled.

He helped each of them to their feet and motioned for them to precede him. He rode Hollister's horse and led the horse the girl had been riding. The stirrups on that horse were much too short.

The heat was increasing even up where there was tree-shade. Miles southward down around the Ruby territory and throughout the land it would be uncomfortably hot, and this was not even summertime yet. It had been Jameson's experience that when it gets so hot this early in the season, it rained. He hoped it would this time. So did everyone else. Not just because rainfall would cool things off for awhile, and not entirely because water would also keep the native grasses growing a bit longer, but also because rainfall lessened the peril from brush fires, the curse of every drying-out cow-country.

When they got back to the spring, and the flour sack, Jameson untied their arms and emptied the sack in front of them. He was not hungry, but he had known they would be. As he squatted and rolled a smoke, he knew the girl was looking at him once again. When he lit up, he turned and said, "Nellie; no one expected you to help him. Least of all Marshal Whitney."

Hollister raised sunken eyes. "You've seen him?"

"Yeah. He got back from the border. Like I warned you about going down there, he had an ambush set up. Anyway, I got the feeling he didn't like it at all, that your daughter busted you out of my jailhouse."

Hollister chewed, swallowed, then said, "Where is he now?"

As far as Jameson knew Whitney was still back in town. He eyed his prisoner thoughtfully. "That man has got the Indian-sign on you, Mister Hollister. Every time you mentioned his name you act like you expect him to jump out from behind a rock."

"That's exactly what I expect him to do, Deputy. That's exactly how Whitney operates. He's as clever as a coyote, and twice as deadly as a rattlesnake. I'm surprised you haven't heard of him down here."

The girl said, "If you turn my father over to Marshal Whitney my father will never get back to Colorado alive."

Jameson glanced over at her. She was indeed very pretty. "If Whitney was all that bad, miss, I suppose we would have heard of him down here."

She sniffed. "You don't believe me?"

"Give me one reason why Whitney would want to kill your pappy, when from Ruby on back to Durango he can keep your pappy in chains and there can't possibly be any trouble."

"Because," the pretty schoolteacher said bleakly, "in case you hadn't heard, Deputy, there is an added bounty of two hundred dollars for bringing back escapees from Durango prison, and if they are brought in dead, there is no delay at all in collecting the bounty."

Jameson started to scoff then he caught the look he was getting from Chuck Hollister. The prisoner soberly nodded his head. "It's the gospel-truth, Deputy," he stated quietly.

Jameson was not unaware of a number of unique situations within the law, and it was rather general knowledge that prison-escapees were viewed within the peace-keeping fraternity as the most dangerous and treacherous of all fugitives, but although he had heard most of the grisly tales of lawmen and bounty-hunters killing prisoners on purpose before hauling them in, he had never really believed it happened very often. To his knowledge, he had never met a lawman who would kill prisoners. Of course, all that indicated was that the lawmen who did make a practice of this did not afterwards talk about it.

Still, as he sat and pondered, waiting for his prisoners to fill up, he admitted to himself that he had met a lot of lawmen he had liked on first sight much better than he had liked Buck Whitney. And that talk of using *Rurales* down along the border was pretty much of a clincher.

He said, "Well; Marshal Whitney isn't going to get his crack at you right off, Mister Hollister. You see, we got a hold on you down here, first. That's for horse-stealing and in Arizona folks look on horse-stealing as a pretty darned serious crime. You could get ten years in prison down here for that." He paused and watched the older man's face getting greyer, and because Jameson was a humane individual first and lawman secondly, he felt sorry for the older man.

He said, "There is something I'd like to hear, Mister Hollister. Twenty-five or so years back you robbed a bank and killed a man..."

Hollister protested but not angrily nor even indignantly. He sounded more wearily resigned, or perhaps hopelessly resigned, when he said, "No, no, no. I didn't kill anyone. I robbed that bank, yes. Maybe there was reason for that. Maybe the reason wasn't good enough. Either way of course it was wrong to rob the bank. But that's not what you want to know about. The man who died in that bank robbery was named Jackson Turner. I did not shoot him. In fact when the clerk who walked out of the backroom and saw me robbing the place reached under his coat for his gun, Turner was leaning down to empty the contents of the safe into the sugar-sack I'd just handed him, and I didn't see the clerk until he turned fully towards me, with his gun hand rising with a gun in it."

Hollister paused, then continued, "I would have fired. I told them at my trial. I would certainly have shot the clerk, but he fired first. The bullet hit Jackson Turner in the forehead where he was beginning to rise up in front of the safe...Deputy; how the hell could I have shot Jackson Turner? I was *behind him*, only the safe was in front of him, and beyond the safe, only the clerk in the doorway of the backroom. Deputy, do you think for one moment that if it had been proved at my trial that I'd murdered Turner that day in the bank, they wouldn't have sentenced me to death by hanging?"

Jameson said nothing for a long while. He motioned for them to arise, now that they had emptied his flour-sack of food and ordered them both to mount one horse as he mounted the other one. It was a fair distance back to town and while it was never Jameson's policy to be in much of a hurry, this time he wanted to reach Ruby before midnight, so he struck out with his prisoners in front, and as they were threading their way back down off the slope towards the lower-down rolling countryside where there were fewer trees and where, eventually, unless they veered to the east side of the stage-road they would end up in the canyon-country, he asked Chuck Hollister why, if what he had said about his crime were true, it had not come out in all the intervening years.

Hollister's answer was succinct. "Who was there to set the record straight, Deputy? Me, a proven outlaw? A dead banker named Turner? A bank-clerk who left the country immediately after my trial and was never heard of again? There were no other witnesses. But as I've already told you-someone had to believe me, back there at the time of the trial, because they didn't hang me, did they?"

Nellie Hollister leaned to study the lawman's face and to afterwards say, Mister Jameson, won't you give my father a chance?"

Jameson's answer to that was abrupt. "It's not up to me. I've already explained to your pappy that all I do is my job-I'll bring him in. That's all."

She replied to that with considerable bitterness. "That's not going to excuse you, when they shoot him in the back. You'll be equally as guilty as Whitney will also be. Sticking your head in the sand won't absolve you at all. Being cowardly is perhaps an even worse crime."

That annoyed Jameson. "Cowardly? How is doing my job being cowardly? I take risks every time I go after someone like your paw!"

She glared. "Not that kind of cowardice, Deputy. Moral cowardice." She mimicked him: "All I do is my job." She continued to glare. "Yes indeed; all you do is your job-hand my father over to a man who is notorious for bringing them back dead-not alive-because you are too morally cowardly to face up to the greater issue, which is simply that not only has my father already paid for robbing that bank with twenty years of life, but now he is going to be murdered for trying to escape so that he won't rot in prison!"

Chapter Seven

Jameson got them back to his jailhouse before midnight, which was about as he planned things. He locked them in without any further conversation with either of them, went to his room at the boardinghouse and slept like a log until dawn, then he went out back to the bath-house, scrubbed hard, put on clean attire and after shaving and greasing his boots he went down to the café for breakfast- the first morning customer, which had been his custom for several years. Long enough, in fact, so that when he entered Leslie West had his cup of coffee ready, with her usual smile.

"You got the child back," she exclaimed, and stood hands on hips waiting to have this confirmed.

Jameson sat down and reached for his cup. "Yeah, I brought her back; brough them both back last night. The girl and her paw."

The coffee was, as usual, both fragrant and delicious. He smiled upwards at the beautiful woman. "I don't know how you do it."

Leslie West was not in the mood for compliments. She turned towards her cooking area as she said, "I'll make up a try for them. By the way, Lincoln, what is their name."

"Hollister. Charles Hollister and Nellie. He's wanted in Colorado for escaping from prison. She's wanted right here for stealing a horse from Murray."

Leslie turned in the doorway of her cooking area. "How do you steal anything from Murray who probably only stole it first!"

"Leslie; just get my damned breakfast will you, please!"

"Well you know it's the truth. Murray Foster never bought a horse at the asking price in his life."

"That don't make him a horse-thief, Leslie."

She went beyond the curtain with the improbable big blue flowers. He rolled and lit his first smoke of the day, and when Pete Clifford walked in looking as bearded and unsmiling as usual, Jameson nodded and turned back to his coffee.

Clifford sat like a massive, hunched carving and read some papers he had brought to breakfast with him. Like most of the single men in Ruby he used Leslie West's café as his mealtime-office. If he'd had a wife, he probably would have acted the same way over her kitchen table.

Eventually he looked up and said, "By the way, Lincoln, that federal lawman was looking for you last night, and when I told him you'd left town he got pretty upset."

Jameson nodded his appreciation for this information-which he was not the least bit pleased to hear.

"Where did you get off the coach?" asked Clifford, "and how did you get back?"

Leslie brought Jameson's breakfast and went on down to Pete Clifford with coffee and a big smile. He did not quite smile back but his eyes brightened perceptibly. Maybe big, handsome Leslie West was more than just the best cook around to the single men of Ruby.

Jameson did not have to answer those questions put to him by the stage company's local boss. He got busy eating and a few moments later Leslie brought Pete's breakfast and that seemed to make him forget most other things.

Only when Leslie brought out the meal tray and had Jameson sign for it did Pete Clifford's interest rise up again, but this time he had no chance to start up their conversation again. Leslie went around to hold the door for Jameson, and he marched directly across the road.

Up in front of the cantina on the east side of the road another man stared. He stopped in mid-stride, watched Jameson enter his jailhouse, and the observer stood looking after Jameson for a couple of seconds after the lawman had closed the jailhouse door behind him. Then the compact, thick and dark-eyed observer continued his way down to the café. He would not have to go over to the jailhouse to find out those plates and saucers and pots on that big tray Jameson has hastened into the jailhouse with. In fact, he would probably get a better response from the handsome woman at the café anyway. Whitney had pretty much well decided that Jameson did not like him.

It was a slightly overcast morning, for which those who took time to notice were thankful. It was cool for a change and in fact that thin, soiled veil of overcast which stretched from north to south above the town was very likely the result of so much marked heat over the past few days. Ordinarily too much unseasonal heat in springtime presaged rainfall. No one would have objected.

Inside the thick-walled jailhouse, however, where changes in the outside temperatures had to be drastic or they made no impression at all, Jameson was leaning in the corridor of his cell-room trying to get something settled in his mind. He was speaking to the older man, Chuck Hollister, who was in turn sipping Leslie West's coffee as though it were ambrosia, when he said, "If there was a doubt in the jury's mind that you maybe didn't kill that banker, sure as hell there would be something about it in your record at the prison, and that being so, why didn't they parole you after maybe ten or fifteen years? Mister Hollister; seems to me there's something strange here."

Hollister glanced up. "Nothing is strange about keeping men in prison. I could cite you a dozen reasons why they are kept there, and the least one of them is that it simply becomes habit, while another one is that Durango is funded according to headcount; if the prison population falls below a certain number the wages and other perquisites of the men who run the place are..."

"Oh hell," mumbled Jameson, interrupting the older man. "I'd expect that unreasonable crap from another fugitive, but not from you. Now tell me-why didn't you appeal? What did the parole board say? Sure as hell you were entitled to a parole hearing after a few years."

From the opposite cell Nellie Hollister said, "He came up for the hearings, Deputy, and was turned down each time because his crime was murder, first, and robbery, second. They said they did not parole murderers."

Someone entered the office from out front. Jameson heard the door open and close. He straightened up and walked forward, to be met with a thick, oaken man starting through on down into the cell room.

Jameson barred the way. "Not visiting time," he told the Deputy U.S. Marshal, and herded him back up out of the cell room, closed and barred the door after him and went over to the desk as Buck Whitney stood wide-legged, frowning his dislike or disapproval.

Whitney said, "You got 'em!"

Jameson would not have denied it in any case. "They are down there eating breakfast."

"The girl too?"

"Yeah."

"I'll wire Denver for another warrant. Meanwhile you keep her and this time..." He went to a chair and dropped down. "How the hell did you get them back?"

"Just luck," answered Jameson and eyed the rather swarthy thicker man. "Is this all you do-hunt them down?"

Whitney smiled bleakly. "I'm better at it than most. I used to have a regular beat like most other deputy marshals, then I turned 'em in one after another." He shrugged, obviously proud of his ability. "Some fellas are better at it than other fellas."

"When you deliver them back up north do you get the bounty? I've always heard federal peace officers aren't allowed to take rewards."

"They aren't," Whitney agreed. "But I can accept travel expenses from either the government or the people

I fetch back a prisoner for. Most prison wardens pay darned good to get someone back. More than travel expenses. You understand?"

"Sure," replied Jameson. "You run them down and bring them back for breaking the law, and you break it by taking underhanded payment for fetching them back."

Whitney's hard, closed expression returned. He leaned to arise as he said, "I got to go make arrangements for the stage trip out of here."

Jameson let him arise and turn towards the door before speaking again. "They aren't going anywhere, Marshal. Not for a while anyway. I made out two warrants on them this morning for horse-stealing. Down here it's a serious offense."

"Murder is more serious," snapped the angered deputy U.S. lawman.

Jameson did not dispute this, he merely said, "I hold folks in my jail for the circuit-rider to pass judgement on. That's the law."

Jameson pursed his lips and glared, then he said, "Are you trying to be funny or are you serious? Those people are my prisoners."

Jameson shook his head very emphatically. "Even if you got an extradition paper from the governor of Arizona Territory, Marshal, you'd still only have a warrant for the old man. Any crime the girl committed, like stealing a horse and also like getting the drop on a lawman to free her father, happened down here, not up in Colorado. You don't have any claim on her at all, that I can see."

Whitney stood turning this over and over in his mind. Eventually he decided to try for a compromise. "All right, Deputy. You can have the girl for your circuit-riding judge. Hand me over her father."

"You got an extradition paper from the Governor of Arizona Territory?"

"Goddamnit," exploded the federal officer. "I'll tell you what this amounts to, Deputy. Obstructing justice and by god that happens to be a serious crime from where I come from."

Jameson arose. "Just show me the paper saying it's all right for you to take Chuck Hollister out of Arizona and I'll gladly hand him over. Otherwise, I got more important things to do than stand here all morning arguing."

Clearly, Marshal Whitney did not have an extradition writ. Not many law officers used them and in most cases for a fact they were not required. Peace officers worked together throughout the states, as well as throughout the various territories, their clear objective being to suppress crime by the best and most expeditious manner, looking the other way in many instances to bypass what they considered formalities and technicalities. Obviously that had been Whitney's intention and quite probably if Jameson had not become suspicious of the federal officer, had not already formed a personal dislike of the man, it might still have happened that way between them. Now, however, it was clear to Marshal Whitney no such accommodations was going to be obtained.

He stood a long-time eyeing Jameson, then he turned and stomped out of the office with no more argument. He had several options, and Jameson was sure he knew them all.

The most obvious option was of course to try and get an extradition writ from the governor's office. The clear difficulty here was that since Ruby did not possess a telegraph office, Marshal Whitney would have to write a letter, then would have to wait around town for maybe a week or ten days before receiving an answer-which just might not be favorable.

Another option was to write the Durango, Colorado, authorities and have them request the extradition writ through formal channels, which might in fact be successful, but that way Whitney was going to have to wait around Ruby even longer.

For Jameson, the dilemma was even more complex though, because he had actually not made up his mind about a personal course of action. He was skeptical of the things Hollister had told him, but even if he had not had doubts, if in fact he had believed every word, he still would not be in a position to do much. He could hold Nellie Hollister. He had figured that out the previous night, and he could try to run a bluff on that horse-theft charge against her father but being able to make a horse-theft take precedence over murder was a very unlikely probability.

Basically, he did not trust Buck Whitney whether or not he was a federal peace officer. He did not really believe Whitney would murder Hollister before delivering him to the people up at Durango, but he was skeptical of Whitney nonetheless. Also, his private opinion was that for someone to serve twenty years or more in prison for a bank robbery was about the limit, especially if the bandit had not got away with anything and if he had not in fact killed anyone during the commission of his crime.

But Jameson's job was not to make the law nor to personally interpret its judgements. All he was supposed to do was exactly what he had told the Hollisters; bring them in.

On the other hand, no one had ever accused Jameson of being a rock-hard, book-tough, iron-fisted enforcer, either. In fact, pretty much the opposite had been said many times of Jameson.

He was not particularly happy about quarrelling with Whitney. Federal law took precedence over just about any other variety of law, and without a doubt Buck Whitney would write a number of letters to various influential agencies and people about the disobedient deputy sheriff down at Ruby, Arizona Territory. He would certainly write one of those letters of outrage to the Territorial Governor and to Jameson's boss, the County Sheriff over at the county seat.

Murray Foster walked in just as Jameson was arriving at his personal opinion. He turned on Murray and said, "I was looking for a damned job when I walked into this one."

This happened to be the second time he had caught Murray unprepared with a sudden outburst. The livery-man feebly grinned, groped his way to a chair, sank down and said, "I'm as obliged as all hell to get that pair of stolen horses back, Lincoln, and I got to commend you for bringing them back in almost as good shape as when they were taken."

Jameson scowled, "Why thank me for the condition they're in? All I did was fetch them back. You want to thank the person who was responsible for caring for them? Come along, then." He took Murray down into his cell-room and halted in front of the girl's cell.

Murray stared at the girl. He stroked his unshaven jaw and looked at Jameson, then turned back for another and much longer look at the girl. "Her?" he demanded of Jameson. "That there handful of a girl took my horses?"

"Yes," the deputy replied, and jerked a thumb. "To help this old gaffer over here to escape from Durango prison after he'd served twenty years and more for trying to rob a bank."

Murray turned and eyed Chuck Hollister who was sitting disconsolately on his cell-bunk. Murray studied Hollister as he said, "Lincoln; he didn't get nothing? He just tried to rob a bank?"

"Ask him, don't ask me, Murray, I wasn't there."

Murray Foster turned fully towards Chuck Hollister. "Well, mister," he enquired, "did you make it with some money or didn't you?"

"No, sir; I wasn't able to get away. I handed over a sugar-sack to be filled from the safe, and I never even saw that sugar-sack again, mister. After that they commenced yelling and shooting out in the road and I had to toss out my gun and surrender."

Murray leaned a moment on Hollister's cell-front then he pulled back slowly to stand erect and face Jameson again. "What horses got stolen yesterday?"

Jameson stared. "Your horses and you damned well know it."

"No sir, Deputy Jameson, there was no such thing. They're back in my barn, ain't they? Then they aren't stolen...And besides, look at that little girl. Why, Lincoln, she's no more than sixteen or seventeen. Slip of a little lady and pretty as a speckled bird...I loaned them those horses."

"You told me......!"

"I got a bad memory. I always have had a bad memory and you can ask anyone around town. I plumb forgot I loaned them those two horses." Murray pushed past heading up out the cell-room. "Put that in your report!" he averred as he disappeared up into the front office on his way out of the building.

Chapter Eight

Even a miracle-worker couldn't help the Hollisters if Providence in the form of Murray Foster refused, because without a complaint against them for horse-stealing, there would be no charge against them in Arizona Territory.

Jameson went after Murray and nailed him over in front of Leslie West's place. Leslie was washing the window nearby and when Jameson said, "Damn you, Murray, you listen to me," Leslie became just as attentive as did the liveryman.

"I've got a complaint made out on my desk," explained Jameson. "When you sign it I can then hold both the old man and his daughter."

Leslie stared with an expression of disbelief as Murray set his jaw in stubborn opposition. "I'm not going to sign a damn thing," he told Jameson, "just so you can keep that pretty little lady in your stinking jailhouse."

"My jailhouse is not stinking," exclaimed the deputy. "Now you listen to me, you old leather-brained horse-thief. I can't hold the Hollisters-the people who stole your horses-unless I have a formal complaint and a signed warrant. Murray, if there is no such legal paper they can walk out of my jailhouse and that Deputy U.S. Marshal will be waiting. He has a hell of a reputation for arriving at destinations with dead prisoners. I don't know anything about that, all I know is that I've got to have a legal excuse for holding them. You've got to sign that complaint."

Murray frowned. "What in the hell are you so fired up about holding these folks for, Lincoln? If it's because of that little slip of a girl you'd ought to be ashamed of yourself."

Leslie came over closer to listen, ostensibly washing the café's front window.

"That child," went on Murray, "can't be a day older than fifteen. And there you stand, a man well along in his..."

"You damned idiot," exclaimed the lawman. "I want to hold the girl so that lousy federal marshal can't take her. That's all I got in mind for her. As for her father-well-it's a long story. I'd like to be able to hang on to him and maybe get the governor to appoint an investigation committee or something. Maybe he'd never have to go back to Durango. All I need, Murray, is your lousy signature."

Leslie West marched up and fixed Murray Foster with a glittering stare.

Murray chuckled uneasily. He slapped Jameson lightly on the shoulder. "Of course. I was just funning with you. Of course I'll sign that there complaint." He took the arm of the deputy and stepped down off the duckboards on his way back in the direction of the jailhouse. From the middle of the road he looked over his shoulder to be certain Leslie was not in hearing distance, then looked forward again as he said, "I felt sorry for the old man. Sorrier for the little slip of girl, mind you, because she doesn't belong in no one's jailhouse, but I can tell you for a damned fact, Lincoln, I can sympathize with the man."

As they were entering the jailhouse the lawman gestured towards his desk. "Just sign. I'm sure the Hollisters will settle for that, and you can keep your sympathy."

"Of course I'll sign. First, could I go back and look at that little girl one more time?"

Jameson found the papers amid his cluttered desk, shoved them over and rigidly pointed. "Sign, that's all you're over here for you lecherous old goat."

Murray squinted. "What kind of an old goat, for Christ sake?"

Jameson shoved a pencil into Murray's hand and balled up a knotty, scarred fist.

Murray sighed, then leaned down to examine the place for his signature and signed with a flourish. As he was handing back the pencil he smiled with pride. "You ever see a finer signature? Did you ever in your life see a nicer set of curlicues, Lincoln?" He smiled and beamed.

"That's all I can do. Sign painter who came through about ten, twelve years ago, taught me how to sign my name one night after I cleaned him out at poker. Of course I can't write or anything like that, nor read, but..."

"You can't read?" asked the deputy and grabbed Murray by the arm to lead him out front in the roadway before releasing him. "Don't you tell a soul that, Murray. Not a soul. You understand?"

"Sure I understand. What's so terrible about being unable to read and write? I know a whole wagonload of folks like that."

"Because, you rockhead, if that Deputy U.S. Marshal finds out, my warrant and complaint will be invalid. When a man signs something he can't read and hasn't been read to him, the law takes the view that he's probably been hoodwinked into signing. Whatever else you do, Murray, don't let that damned federal peace officer know you're illiterate."

"For the Lord's sake stop stewing will you," Murray exclaimed. "I'm not going to tell that federal lawman." Murray pushed past Lincoln and went hiking towards his barn. He muttered something to himself and walked the last two dozen yards with both fisted hands rammed deeply into his trouser pockets. Murray was not proud of his illiteracy. He was not exactly overwhelmed with shame about it because there were an awful lot of other folks around who'd never learned to read or write and do sums and all, but he would just as soon the subject were not brought up again.

Marshal Whitney emerged from the general store with a pouch of chewing tobacco in his hand. He saw

Jameson. In fact, they exchanged a look, and this of course made it just about impossible for them not to speak since they were close enough for it.

Jameson said, "If you're going to send telegrams to the governor and to the authorities up at Durango-and over to the President in his White House for all I know-you'd better be getting astraddle of a good horse, or you'll never make it up to Sulphur Springs which is the nearest town with a telegraph office in time for your message to get out soon."

"They'll get out soon enough," growled the federal officer, and turned to depart northward as he also said, "Don't get too happy with yourself, Deputy. You don't know Buck Whitney."

That was of course true, but it also happened to be true that Jameson was *beginning* to know Buck Whitney; was at least beginning to suspect that some of the things Chuck Hollister had said about Whitney might indeed be true.

Henry Cooper came forth from his store to glance up the road after Marshal Whitney, then to turn towards Jameson and wag his head. "I didn't know we had a U.S. Marshal in town."

"*Deputy* U.S. Marshal," stated the deputy, also glancing northward. "We've had them here before."

"He was just telling me that you've got a pair of federal offenders over at the jailhouse."

Jameson turned back to face the storekeeper. "I never figured he was stupid, Henry, and now I'm convinced of it. He found out that you're apart of the town council. He's softening you up in his feud with me."

Cooper looked distressed. 'What are you feuding with a federal marshal for?"

"For one thing he wants a prisoner of mine, a young girl, and she hasn't committed a crime against the federal law. In fact, Henry, she hasn't committed any crime that she can be successfully prosecuted for. I locked her up for stealing a couple of horses from Murray, and now he swears he loaned her the horses, and hell, he never saw her until I brought her back with his horses."

Cooper peered perplexedly at the lawman. "That sounds too damned complicated for me." He waited a moment, evidently arriving at a private opinion, then he said, "Maybe you're right. Maybe I let that federal officer impress me. All right, Lincoln, it's your headache." Henry Cooper turned and re-entered his store and behind him Jameson sarcastically said, "Thanks, Henry," and also turned way.

Jameson went across to his jailhouse office and was finishing a letter when Pete Clifford, the stagecoach company supervisor, walked in and nodded his head as he looked around for a chair.

"Someone ran off five head of company horses last night," Pete reported, and oddly enough he showed no great agitation. "I didn't learn about it until a short while ago when the fella who rides out every day or two to look at our livestock in pasture came back in and told me. He looked high and low. They are gone, Lincoln, stolen. Someone drove them out the pasture gate and closed the gate after them."

"Your hostler picked up the sign?" asked Jameson.

"Yeah, but he's pretty young. He doesn't know how to follow tracks very well-unless they're as plain as the nose on his face. All he told me was that the riders went south, which would be about what most folks would suspect. Mexicans, sure as hell. Lousy Mexican raiders again. I thought after we hanged the last three it would stop but I guess that was wrong, eh?"

Jameson ignored the question. "Last night?"

Burly and unsmiling Pete Clifford fidgeted a little in the chair. "Well; I never saw the tracks, Lincoln. All I'm going by is what the hostler told me."

"And you just said he wasn't too wise."

"I said he wasn't much of a tracker; but all right, he's not too smart either...Maybe the damned horses were stolen later. Maybe they were taken out sometime this morning. All I can tell you for a fact is that they aren't out there now and there are some tracks around the gate to show they were driven out. Maybe this morning. Only it doesn't make much sense to steal horses in daylight."

Jameson could have argued that point. A lot of horses were stolen in broad daylight, especially out of pastures which were miles from a town or from a nearby ranch. Instead he simply said, "I'll go out and look around." He leaned to offer the sealed envelope he had completed filling just prior to the other man's arrival. "Stick that in the outgoing mail, will you?"

After Pete Clifford had departed Jameson sighed. He had ridden after a lot of horse-thieves in his time as local deputy, and if they had much of a start and were well-mounted, and were heading due south to the border, he had caught very, very few of them. What was required to discourage those Mex raids up over the line was co-operation south of the border, and that was simply not forthcoming. In Mexico along the thousand-mile border the prevailing feeling had always been one of animosity, even though it was usually well concealed. Anything which could be stolen north of the line and delivered south of the line, was considered legitimately Mexican, and there had been innumerous instances of Mexican authorities not just making a point of looking the other way when pursued horse and cattle thieves came charging through, but those same authorities had usually managed to hamper the gringo pursuit in any way that they could in order for the thieves to successfully elude apprehension.

Jameson's preoccupation with the stage company's stolen horses was primarily based upon just how much head-start the border-jumpers had. If they had indeed driven off the horses last night, then there was almost no chance at all Jameson would be able to recover them. He probably would be unable to even see their dust.

If they made their raid this morning, say perhaps only a few hours earlier, then Jameson's chances were better. What had to be determined of course, from reading the sign out at the pasture was when, exactly, this raid had actually taken place.

First, he had to go across the road, give Leslie West his key to the cell-room and ask her to feed his prisoners while he was gone. And to also warn her to be very careful because both the Hollisters were accomplished escapists.

Then he had to go down to Murray's place, rig out a horse and head for the stage company's pasture, which was three miles south-east of town, down where the broken country had rather good feed at this time of year.

He found the gate and the tracks. He also thought that hostler for Pete Clifford had not wanted to track the stolen livestock because the tracks were as plain as daylight. There had been no attempt made to hide them as the raiders had turned southward and had kept to the open country.

Amateurs, Jameson decided, or just plain fools. No rustler in his right mind ever remained in open country with his stolen animals if he could avoid it.

The tracks indicated that there had been only three raiders. Instead of the customary heavily-jumping desperadoes, the sign Jameson began following could not have been made by more than three men.

He rode for a solid hour and a half, had no difficulty at all with the sign, and eventually decided he was pursuing fools, experience or not, fools.

They began angling in the direction of the southward coach-road, even, and granting that the travelling over there would be easier and faster it was the height of folly for rustlers to actually employ a public thoroughfare in their flight.

Finally, Jameson drew rein between a pair of red stone boulders, one on each side of the coach-road, as large as a house, and stepping down to roll and light a smoke and to consider things. The horse-thieves were going straight southward. They would not be able to reach the border until the next day but that was obviously where they were heading.

Maybe, along with being fools, they were also strong hearts-men who were full of contempt for gringos and especially for north-americano lawmen. Men willing to take big risks.

It was possible. It was not likely; most border jumpers were as nervous as cats for as long as they were north of the line, but it was possible.

This sort of raid was actually more in the Apache tradition than in the Mexican tradition. The Apaches were more concerned with accomplishments they could brag about. Mexican raiders were less concerned in risk than in making successful raids and getting back below the line as swiftly and as discreetly as possible. Especially when there were only three of them. A big armed band might not be as wary of armed contact with pursuers but three raiders most certainly would be.

Jameson finished the smoke, swung back astride and loped another mile watching the tracks. They overlay all other recent sign upon the coach-raid and were as simple to follow as running water.

Finally, he halted and told his horse something was damned wrong here. He could see dead-ahead for many miles, could in fact see on both sides of the road as well. There was no dust, no indications he was not totally alone down here, and yet the feeling that he was the center of someone else's close interest remained with him.

Then he turned back. The moment he did that he doomed those five stolen horses to sale and use below the border, but as he told himself on the ride back in the direction of Ruby, he probably would not have been able to overtake them anyway.

He had ridden a long way, had used up a lot of time without being aware of it, and by the time he was up where he could make out Ruby's rooftops again the day was close to ending.

He was hungry, his horse was both hungry and thirsty, and Pete Clifford was going to look passively disgusted when Jameson confessed that he had turned back.

Chapter Nine

He was right about Pete Clifford. The way-station manager was in his corral yard when Jameson entered still dusty from riding, and having only moments earlier left his ridden-down animal for Murray to look after.

Clifford the persistent pessimist, said, "You didn't recover them."

"Didn't even see them," confirmed Jameson. "Them or their dust. I've got some friends over the line. I'll send down word for them to keep their eyes open. When the horses show up, maybe we can both go down there and make an identification." Jameson was not very hopeful and it showed.

Pete Clifford considered a jacked-up stage in the center of the yard where several yardmen were conversing as they peered beneath it. "We won't get them back," he mused aloud to Jameson. "I figured that was how it would end up when the lad came back and told me they'd been stolen. Thing is, the company is pretty lucky. Those are the first horses we've lost from around Ruby in about six, seven years, which is a hell of a lot better than things have been for most cow-outfits and freighters around here. That's why I wasn't too upset.... That, and the fact that they only took five head."

"How many head you got in that pasture?" asked the deputy.

"By my last inventory I'd say about thirty-five head."

Jameson stared at Clifford. "Five out of thirty-five?"

The company man agreed. "Yeah; that's what I figured. Five out of thirty-five head isn't bad, is it?"

Jameson agreed and turned to walk back into the late-day afternoon softening early dusk. He had gone first to the stage office. Now, instead of going down to the jailhouse, he angled across until he entered the café. He was hungry. Besides, Leslie would be able to give him the latest report on his prisoners.

She saw him coming from the sparkling-clean roadway window and came forth with a cup of fresh coffee. He smiled at her. "I'm sure going to miss you some day," he said, dropping down at the counter and reaching for the cup.

She looked blankly at him. "Why? Are you going away?"

"No, not that I know of anyway. One of these days some cowman will come along and sweep you off your feet and pack you out to his ranch as his wife. From then he'll be the only fella to get your coffee every day."

She blushed and said, "Oh for heaven's sake!" and turned to get his supper. He halted her at the doorway to her cooking area.

"How are my prisoners?"

She looked steadily at him when she replied. "They are well-fed, if that's what you mean. Otherwise, being locked up in cages like animals..."

"I meant were they well fed and healthy. That's all. Leslie, I'm hungry enough to eat my boots."

"Don't you have a conscience, Lincoln?" she demanded. "That child over there..."

"That child, Leslie, happens to have a full-fledged schoolmarm. She also happens to be tough enough to ride like the wind and outsmart folks with gun in her hand when she wants to...Please, just something to eat."

She balanced in the doorway a moment longer, then disappeared into her cooking area.

Jameson sipped coffee, meticulously hoarded a lot of small scraps in his mind, and suddenly sat up straight on the bench. He had been completely unable to figure out why those thieves had taken only five horses. Rustlers were not hanged one inch higher than for stealing just five of them. In fact, for just three raiders, it would have been better to round up and drive the entire herd with them, and sift out a few along the way to create false sets of followable tracks.

There was a damned good reason for those bandidos to take only five head, then, and he did not believe it was because the thieves were stupid. It had to be based on something other than that.

What?

Leslie returned with a medium-done steak, a big slab of still-hot apple pie, more coffee, and biscuits with butter. As she wordlessly arranged the plates in front of him she carefully avoided looking at him.

He sighed. "Why does it always end in an argument when I come here?"

"It doesn't always!"

"Lately it always has," he affirmed. "Leslie, I'm trying harder than anyone else to keep both the Hollisters from having to go back up to Colorado. We're both on the same side."

"You've got them both in the jailhouse, haven't you?"

He exploded. "For Christ sake, if I didn't have them in there that damned federal marshal would grab them in the roadway and whisk them out of here on the very next..." He suddenly stopped speaking and stared round-eye at her. "Five god damned horses out of thirty-five." He sprang up and lunged for the door, bolted diagonally past the jailhouse on his way back to the stage company's corral yard.

Pete Clifford was not out there, he was in his office. Jameson barged in there a little out of breath. Clifford lifted perplexed, somber dark eyes. "What's wrong?" he asked.

"Why didn't someone take all your horses out of the pasture," demanded Jameson, then did not allow Pete Clifford a chance to reply. "If they had, Pete, if they had taken them all, would you have had enough team-animals here in the corral yard to keep up the stage schedules?"

Clifford leaned back gently in his chair studying the deputy. "No, of course not. We run two coaches out Ruby daily-as you damned well know-one in the morning and one in the afternoon. On the north run because they got to go up through a pass in the mountains, we got to put six horses on the tongue. On the southward runs over flat country, only four horses. We alternate our horses. Work a few and keep them stalled here in town, then turn out the others at the pasture. Without the pasture-livestock, we'd be hamstrung. What is this all about?"

Jameson briefly smiled and turned to depart. "I'm not sure but when I am, I will let you know." He paused at the door to turn and ask one more question. "Did you send that hostler to the pasture today because this was the usual day to ride out there?"

Clifford was looking more baffled than ever as he said, "There isn't any usual day. Someone rides out there every couple of days. At the most every three days, and usually they fetch back some livestock."

"That's not what I asked you. Why did you send him out today?"

"Well, that federal marshal who was in town told me at the tavern last night there's been a lot of raiding in these parts lately."

Jameson said, "Sure; and he thought it might be a good idea for you to keep watch on your pasture."

"Yes. What's wrong with that?"

"He's not from around these parts," Jameson said. "How would he know anything about what's going on in these parts? Who was on the morning coach while I was riding all over hell looking for your damned horses? Who were the passengers?"

"The federal marshal, a travelling salesman named Sutherland, and older fella and a young woman."

Jameson continued to stand there. Whitney had been right as rain when he said Jameson did not know Buck Whitney. Jameson had been duped as neat as it could be done. He had been fooled by Whitney without the federal lawman appearing in the affair at all. If Whitney had appeared Jameson's suspicions would have been aroused, and Buck Whitney had known that.

He finally walked on down to the jailhouse, entered, saw the cell-room door ajar and did not even bother going down there because the ring of keys was hanging upon the door-strap exactly where Whitney had deliberately put it so that Jameson would see it.

This time, he had no trick for getting ahead of the abducted prisoners. Whitney would have known about that also. He was an accomplished lawman.

Jameson rolled a smoke, sauntered into his empty cell-room, closed the two cell doors which had been left open after his prisoners had been taken out, and sauntered back up to the office going over in his head the route of the morning coach and it's approximate location at this time of day.

The stages had dusk-stops all along the line. They would lie over until morning to rest the drivers and passengers, and to also allow the next hitch of horses to be fresh when they were put on the pole the following day.

But there were relay-coaches waiting to push onward and the further north one went the better the stage service got. Even if Jameson rode a horse down and borrowed another one along the way, by morning he would only be where Whitney *had been*. He would not be close to where Whitney was now.

It had been a clever plot. Those Mexicans who had stolen the horses undoubtedly were some of Whitney's *Rurale* friends, and they too had managed their parts very well. They had in fact done it so well they had lured Jameson miles farther southward than he normally would have gone-and that had been part of the scheme.

If the country happened to be one of those cow-ranges where a lawman could race northward exchanging horses at the various contiguous cow-camps as he went, even though it would be a grueling undertaking there was a fair chance he would be able to overtake Whitney and the abducted captives.

But the country was not that kind of cow-range. There were several big cow outfits but there were all miles to the west of town.

Also, if there had been a telegraph facility in Ruby...there wasn't. The nearest one was at the town of Sutherland, fifteen miles north and east. He could make it up there, and he could send telegrams ahead for someone to take Whitney and his captives off the coaches, but unless that was done before they got over the line out of Arizona and into Colorado, Jameson's requests would probably not be honored, and there was also a fine chance that they wouldn't be honored anyway. No one would be enthusiastic about arresting a Deputy U.S. Marshal. To Jameson's knowledge it had never been done. At least he had never heard of it being done.

But there was nothing else to do except sit down and philosophically acknowledge that he had been outsmarted by Buck Whitney, who had probably chuckled all the way northward to the first stage-halt-with his tired and stooped and demoralized prisoner Chuck Hollister , and Nellie Hollister who had actually done nothing she could be prosecuted for, since Murray Foster had refused to say she had stolen two horses from him.

It was a long, tiresome ride to Sutherland but Jameson went down to the liverybarn, got his unused, second horse, and struck out. He told no one where he was going and except for Murray and a couple of loafers down in front of the liverybarn sitting in tree-shade, no one paid much attention to his departure. It was dusk so most folks were home having supper anyway.

He rode northward, but over along the westerly end of town, and once he was clearly aways he eased his horse over into a gentle lope. He could hold the animal to that gait as long as the terrain permitted, but after a while as he encountered some of the up-ended rough terrain which bordered the canyon-country he had to slack off, and this would require a lot more riding than he looked forward to. But there was no way of getting around it.

Even if he had started out right after breakfast, he still would not have been able to reach Sutherland until dusk. Riding the stage-road added several miles to the trip, and cutting across country, through the canyon-country, while it was much shorter, required slow riding.

Nor did he feel very pleased with himself. The more ground he covered, the more thinking he did, the more humiliated and vengeful he felt, and actually Jameson was not ordinarily a vengeful man. But then, neither had he been duped very often, nor so professionally.

He was coming up alongside Buckskin Canyon when he saw a faint dust-banner over at the mouth, but it was not being made by people riding *into* the canyon, it was being made by someone riding *out*.

He watched it because he was interested, but he did not alter his course. He assumed that dust was being made by waggoneers, who were probably striking camp and starting out again. Or possibly wild horses. There was always green feed and water inside the canyon.

Only when he saw the riders did he realize it was not a wagon-band, and while he watched, although they were small in the distance they were swarming out of Buckskin Canyon and swinging around to lope up the east wall, travelling on such a course that unless they, or Jameson altered course, they would meet.

For a mile Jameson was interested. Not the least bit apprehensive, just interested. He did not change course. If those men were mustangers, which seemed possible, they were certainly in the right area for catching a few.

Then, finally, with nothing else to watch and with nothing around which could hold his interest this well, he finally saw something which rang a bell of warning in his head. Those riders were Mexicans. There seemed to be about six or seven of them. It was not just the sombreros and the easy grace of their riding style which identified them to Jameson, it was also the esilla vaqueros-the Mexican saddles-they were riding, which became visible eventually.

The idea struck him like a bow. *Rurales*!

If they had been caught up here by the U.S. authorities it was highly improbable that they would have got back to Mexico alive. But there was no army command ahead of them, there was just Deputy Sheriff Lincoln Jameson, and although he was armed with both a Colt and a booted Winchester and was a good hand with both, he was not the match for six or seven *Rurales.* No solitary rider who had ever existed, was a match for that many *Rurales*.

He swerved his horse and said aloud, "That son of a bitch Whitney!" Then he spent no more time speculating on how well Whitney had planned this entire thing because from now on his life was at stake. Those particular Mexicans trying to prevent him from getting into the broken country on ahead and slightly to the west, were unscrupulously treacherous and absolutely deadly. That was how they were required to be in order to be accepted into their dreaded organization. Particularly up here, in gringo country, they would kill on sight in order to prove that there had been a *Rurale* invasion of U.S. territory.

Fortunately for Jameson, he had been hoarding the resources of his saddlehorse, while the Mexican, having no doubt spied his approach from atop the east wall of Buckskin Canyon before busting out in a dead run to catch him, had been compelled to come farther and therefore to use up more of the strength of their animals.

This one thing was what Jameson decided was going to save his life-if anything could save it!

Chapter Ten

But Jameson also had another factor favorable to his possible survival. He knew this broken, canyon-country as well as anyone else, and those Mexicans probably did not know it at all, since they were not natives of this area.

He studied the oncoming dusk and decided that, as slow as it was progressing down-country from beyond the far-away mountains, whatever happened to him would have happened by the time full darkness could help very much.

He studied the oncoming Mexicans, decided they were fanning out for just one purpose-to cut him off-and he waited until they had to go down into an arroyo and start up the opposite side, before he suddenly turned southward, rowelled his horse and broke over into a steady run in the direction of Buckskin Canyon, which was by this time far behind the pursuing Rurales.

They would not have expected him to turn back instead of trying to outrun them into the broken country on ahead, and if they had spent much time in the canyon-which they no doubt had done since they surely must have come north with those other *Rurales,* the ones who had stolen the stage-company's horses-they knew Buckskin Canyon was a natural trap-a box-canyon with only one way in and out.

As they came laboring up the near side of the arroyo and looked for Jameson, then made him out racing over their own backtrail, the Mexicans paused, rode all together in a little milling group, talked swiftly back and forth for a few moments, then turned back towards Buckskin Canyon. But from here on they favored their livestock. There was no reason for them not to favor it. They were no longer going to have to pursue the gringo to overtake and kill him. All they knew now had to do was walk back over to the mouth of that big canyon with the vertical granite walls, seal off the entrance, and at their leisure send a couple of men ahead to locate and shoot the bottled up gringo.

Jameson rode twisted in the saddle. As soon as he saw how the Mexicans were lining out in their leisurely pursuit of him, he guessed what was in their minds. He smiled to himself. He had no intention of being bottled up in there. He too had explored Buckskin Canyon, and many more times than those *Rurales* had. He knew perfectly well that short of sprouting wings no one could get out, once the entrance to the place was sealed off.

But near the canyon's entrance, along the west wall where thornpin grew, a few spidery little paloverdes grew along with buckbrush and creosote bush, was the little path he had used a week earlier to climb atop the canyon's west wall and wait for Hollister's cooking fire to reveal where the fugitive was encamped.

Actually, that small game-trail, half-hidden as it was, was no secret. Most of the people who were familiar with the vicinity of Buckskin Canyon knew it existed, but it was south of the actual mouth of the canyon, so if someone did not know there actually was a way to get out of the trap before it was too late to escape, they would rush right on past the game-trail. A lot of people had done that over the ears. In fact, Jameson himself had pressed fugitives he had pursued in order to compel them to race past without noticing the game-trail.

It was not particularly well-marked in any case. Some people who had explored the canyon over the years had blithely ridden right on past, but Jameson didn't. He used a big burst of speed to get himself around the curve of east-wall granite beyond the sight of the Mexicans, then he ruthlessly gouged his horse to race directly across the canyon's mouth, up through the yonder paloverdes and underbrush and up the game-trail.

He was forced to haul the horse back down to a walk in order not to raise tell-tale dust. And for as long as the horse plodded steadily along Jameson rode looking rearward, unsure whether he would be able to cross the top-out and be out of sight down the far side before the Mexicans came charging into the mouth of the canyon.

He made it, but only because the Mexicans did not charge up, they walked up, and clearly the only reason they did this was because they were confident they now had Jameson bottled up in the canyon.

In fact he dismounted part way down the trail, walked back and lay belly-down in the cooling shale to watch. The *Rurales* came around the granite wall in a sloppy formation and neglected to even glance in any direction but the one dead ahead of them. They rode up into the canyon without a sound. Jameson felt hair along the back of his head rise up as he watched the silent, methodical, utterly cold and deadly way those men rode into the canyon, spreading out so as to close off every possible route out of the canyon for anyone trapped up ahead of them.

He had never actually seen *Rurales* in action before but he knew from watching their efficient, experienced advance that this was a typical no-quarter maneuver they were now employing, and when he had seen enough and turned to go back down to his horse, the animal turned, saw him coming and did something it had never done before-it neighed at him.

The sound carried through the lazily settling late evening clarion-clear. Jameson had no illusions about those men down in the canyon not having heard, nor did he fool himself by believing they were not horsemen enough to understand what that horse-call had been about.

He ran down, yanked up the reins, flung himself astride and booted the horse on down the remainder of the game-trail to flatter country.

He was not especially worried-yet. He knew more places to hide throughout this broken country than almost anyone else; he certainly knew more places than his pursuers knew.

What he had to do was stay well out of carbine-range. The *Rurales* would not make another run at him without firing. Now, they knew perfectly well that he understood who they were and what they were trying to do-kill him!

The horse was strong, and he had recovered from the earlier race, so now as Jameson checked him up just a little in order to conserve enough driving power so that if he had to suddenly make a run for it there would be something left in the horse to run with, he kept looking over his shoulder. When the first *Rurale* topped out back where Jameson was half a mile ahead, and by the time that first one had reached the base of the game-trail with his friends strung out behind him, Jameson was more than a mile beyond. Carbines could reach that far, but never accurately, and as the Mexicans strung out at the base of the trail to begin another of their wide sweeps overland, Jameson's horse got a little slack in the reins and shot ahead to shortly widen the distance by more than a mile and a half.

Jameson felt safe, at least for the time being. Providing nothing happened to the horse under him he was confident he could reach the vicinity of Sutherland before midnight, and those Mexicans would never get any closer than they now were. The way he devised to do this, he began shortly to put into execution.

He entered a deep arroyo riding northward. At the bottom he reversed his course and loped southward a mile. Of course in daylight the *Rurales* would have read the sign the moment they also went down into the arroyo. As things now stood, although there was still considerable evening light up above, down where there had been no sunlight for hours, at the bottom of the arroyo, tracks were a lot less readily visible.

Jameson climbed out of the arroyo continued southward for another half-mile, then he turned almost due west. He knew where a cow-camp was five miles father out. It was not his intentions to stop there, to rout up the rangemen to help him in a fight with the Mexicans. He did not want to halt that long. But what he had in mind came close to creating an alliance against the *Rurales.*

Deputy U.S. Marshal Whitney was not the only one capable of organizing a scheme.

He allowed his horse to lope slowly until it had recovered from the earlier race, then he pulled down to a walk. By the time he saw the Mexicans far back he was confident enough to loop both reins and methodically roll a smoke, light it, and watch the pursuit, wearing a small smile.

He suddenly recalled the meal he had bolted from, back at Leslie West's café. It was less the missed opportunity to eat a medium-rare steak cooked as only Leslie could cook a steak, than it was the look which must have been on her face when he abruptly leapt up from her counter and raced out of there.

Women could be very reasonable. He blew smoke, sighed resignedly because he knew she was going to be angry when he got back, and twisted ahead when his horse missed a lead, its attention obviously snagged up ahead.

The horse must have picked up the scent of other horses because as far as Jameson could determine there was nothing ahead but a slight levelling-off of the badly broken and up-ended country.

He knew for a fact where that cow-camp would be. There was an old marking-ground out there in a slight, broad depression where grass grew and where a small creek came down out of the northward lifts and rises.

The horse's interest became more and more centered upon something ahead, but by now visibility was becoming far too poor for Jameson to be able to make out anything. Then a horse nickered up ahead, so close in fact that Jameson started in the saddle. He had ridden almost into the hobbled remuda of the using cow-camp horses. It had not been his intention to get this close but now that he could make out more and more pairs of little ears coming up out of the grass, he halted, stubbed out his smoke atop the saddlehorn, peered ahead until he could dimly discern a feeble supper fire out there in the swale, on the far side of a wagon, where those range men were unsuspectingly getting ready to eat, then he twisted to look back where the *Rurales* were coming, and although it was now getting extremely difficult to see that far back, he could hear them, and that was all he had to be certain of.

He lifted out his Colt, walked his horse northward away from the hobbled remuda, waited until the sound of on-coming riders were clearly audible, then he fired into the air twice, fired one over the top of that wagon down yonder, and let out an ear-splitting howl as he swung and fired off the remaining slugs from his sixgun in the direction of the *Rurales*.

He did not race away, but he loped his horse for a mile before altering gait, and then he dropped down to walk to let the horse pick its own way through the increasing darkness while he sat sideways looking back and listening.

Those range men had come boiling out of their camp armed and fiercely indignant about what they clearly assumed was a raid being made upon their remuda. There was gunfire from both sides. What the *Rurales* thought was anyone's guess, but by this time it must have occurred to several of them that they had been duped, had been deliberately led into this battle with the range men while the individual they had been pursuing escaped through the night.

Jameson told his horse it was a lot of luck, and a little commonsense utilization of the rough and unfriendly countryside, which had saved both of them.

He listened to the skirmishing back yonder and drew satisfaction from it; he had paid someone back, at least in part, for what they had attempted to do to him, but the primary target of his need for revenge was even farther away than ever. He was convinced of that all the way over to Sutherland, which was situated in kinder, more gentle country although it was possible to see the canyon-country from Sutherland, out a few dozen miles to the west and east, and southward only a mile or two. It was from the south that the solitary rider came forth from hushed darkness, crossing the intervening grassland to enter Sutherland and ride up to its liverybarn where he rattled the harness-room door until a blearly-eyed hostler came forth looking so disgusted Jameson almost smiled despite his weariness.

He flipped a half-cartwheel to the older man. "He deserves the best hay and grain you got, partner, and a dry stall, and in the morning a good cuffing with a stiff brush."

The hostler looked more annoyed than ever. Clearly, as a lifelong horseman, one at least fifteen years older than Jameson, he did not require anyone's instructions about how to look after an animal which had obviously been ridden hard this night.

Jameson said, "Where does the telegrapher live?"

"In the rooms off the back of his shop," muttered the nighthawk and tuned to lead the horse away.

Jameson's footfalls echoed loudly throughout the slumbering town. Except for one smoking old lantern in the center of town, hanging from a wire stretched from a storefront on the east side of the road and from a storefront on the west side, Sutherland was dark throughout.

Jameson did not carry a watch so he could only guess about the time, until he had made such a racket out front of the telegrapher's office that the man came stamping through to fling open the door and say, "What the hell is wrong with you, mister? Don't you realize it's damned near two o'clock in the morning?" This telegrapher was not the typically small, older type with a green eyeshade on his forehead. He was half a head taller than Jameson and just as wide, and he looked to be nor more than perhaps twenty-five. Clearly, when this man frowned and sounded disagreeable it behooved folks to look a little out.

Jameson tapped the badge on his shirtfront. "I'm from Ruby. Deputy down there. I've got to send a telegram to the towns up along the border with Colorado, immediately. I'm sorry about routing you out like this, but there just was no other way, and mister if you think getting out of bed is tough, try it the way I've just done it- in the saddle and without any sleep since last night."

The telegrapher threw his door wide open and turned to light a lamp, but his expression did not change much. He removed a canvas from his sending-key and without a word shoved a lined tablet and a chewed pencil towards Jameson. As the lawman leaned in guttering lamplight to form a message the telegrapher cleared his key, waited, and when it seemed he had the right-of-way he turned, accepted the message from Jameson and leaned over as he read it. His expression smoothed out, eventually. He looked up and said, "A real deputy marshal did all that?"

Jameson smiled. "If you're interested I'll tell you all about it, friend, *after* you send the message."

The telegrapher was experienced at his trade, and while Jameson watched and marveled, a thick shadow came into the roadside doorway and loitered, hat shoved back, thick thumbs hooked in his belt. He was town Marshal Beau Greene, and when he recognized the other man in the office with the telegrapher, he sighed and became satisfied to just stand there until the message had been sent. But originally, when he'd heard all that ruckus out front when Jameson had been rattling the office door, Marshal Greene hadn't been so sure someone wasn't trying to break into one of the roadside stores and perhaps commit a burglary.

Chapter Eleven

The big telegrapher and the town marshal listened to Jameson's story with solemn faces, then the telegrapher went out back to make some coffee and the town marshal asked about the Mexicans, his clear objective being to round up a posse even at this ungodly hour and go back down there. He seemed to be as anti-border-jumper as everyone else in central and southern Arizona. With some, it was plainly a strong, endemic dislike of Mexicans, and there was enough reason for this sentiment throughout all the border territories and states to make certain that in each town at least one person in authority had it. In Sutherland, it could have been Town Marshal Beau Greene although his sentiments now seemed more nearly based upon justifiable indignation about Mexican *Rurales* being up over the line trying to murder someone.

When the telegrapher returned with three cups and a small, soiled tin pot with coffee in it, he looked enquiringly at the constable. "Say the word, Beau, and I'll go round up the poker gang from the saloon. Ought to be eight or ten of us. Shouldn't need much more, should we?"

The telegraphers receiver began to clatter. Marshal Greene got no chance to reply to the telegrapher because this interruption caught and held the attention of all three of them although only one of them knew what it signified.

The telegrapher went over, hunched at his table to listen, and when Jameson was certain no one could make any sense of that busy little chatter, the telegrapher cut in to tap out something, then to sit down with the chewed pencil and the lined tablet and begin transcribing.

Marshal Greene shrugged, drank coffee and strolled to his former place in the doorway. Over there, he leaned to study the dark sky. Evidently what he saw was not promising because he turned and said, "Deputy, I guess by the time we get up a posse and bust down there, those cowmen will have either been wiped out, or the Mexicans will have. I know that marking-ground. It's a damned good six miles south of here. Belongs to an old cuss named McCallister, and he's just about as disagreeable an old man as you'll ever run across."

Jameson also knew McCallister and knew the old cowman's disposition, but he had always managed to get along out there, probably mainly because he rarely ever rode to the McCallister outfit.

In any event, McCallister's disposition was not the issue. "If I can get a fresh horse from the liverybarn," Jameson said. "I'll go back down there. It was my doings; I led those Mexicans right up to that camp to get them off my trail. I owe somebody down there some help, if they still need it, and if they don't I sure as hell owe them some thanks."

Marshal Greene said, "We'll go. Don't get the wrong notion, Deputy, we'll get up a posse here in town and we'll go down there. But I'd feel better if I knew it would be sunrise or at least dawnlight by the time we get into that broken country. I've been shot at from among the trees and rocks and little canyons so many times in my life I just naturally got a bad feeling about charging into trouble in the dark."

Both lawmen turned as the telegrapher leaned back studying a paper in his hand. He shot them a look. "This here is from the wireless feller up at Clayton. He received my message a while ago, and called back to say he hadn't checked with their lawman at Clayton yet, but he knew for a fact a coach had arrived in town this evening from down around Ruby and it had a sick fella in it. They took him off and put him in a bed in the hotel, and the federal deputy marshal riding with this fella had a fit for their lawman up there not allowing the sick man to be taken on."

The telegrapher leaned to hand the slip of paper to Beau Greene. "Read it and give me your response," he said, acting as though Jameson were not even in the room, which may have been justifiable, after all the telegrapher did not have the authority to take any initiative at all in this bizarre affair, but his friend the town marshal did.

Greene handed the paper to Jameson, then went over to the doorway to look at the sky again. When Jameson finished reading Beau Greene said, "We got a morning stage out of here bound for points north, including Clayton, and if you want to be on it, Deputy, you go right ahead. Me and the boys here in town will go south and look around down at McCallister's outfit. If we catch a Mexican or two we'll hold them for invasion, and you won't have to worry about it." Greene turned. "One thing: when you reach Clayton which you ought to do by tomorrow night-tonight I meant to say-telegraph us back down here and let us know how you made out arresting a federal deputy marshal. We'll let you know how we made out with the Mexicans." The town marshal turned and nodded at the telegrapher as though to signify it would be all right for the telegrapher to do whatever the deputy from Ruby suggested.

With the way clear, Jameson wrote out another message, this time to the telegrapher up at Clayton. He was to ask the Clayton lawman to say absolutely nothing to Deputy U.S. Marshal Buck Whitney about the impending arrival of the lawman from Ruby, and he was to hold that ill passenger off the stage if his name happened to be Hollister.

As the large, younger man took this message to read it before transcribing it, Beau Greene thought it might be a good idea for Jameson to go with him over to the corralyard, where the hostlers would be stirring by now, since it was a little past four in the morning, and make certain he could get passage on the northbound morning stage.

Not only were the yardmen already at work over there, but the stage company's Sutherland representative was also up and active. Beau Greene left Jameson to go briskly hiking back towards the telegraph office. His last words to Jameson had to do with desire to get his posse on horseback as quickly as possible.

Sutherland's stage-line superintendent was a youngish, different from Pete Clifford down at Ruby in that he smiled, affably talked with Jameson, and when the coach was ready to roll finally, personal escorted Jameson to a seat before the rig left the yard to park at roadside and take on regular stowage including several light freight, and three more passengers.

One passenger was a travelling dentist. He kept two of his valises inside with him rather than risk having them bounced over the side from atop the stage.

Another passenger was a fiercely bearded immigrant with dark, gypsy eyes and a burly build. He had a companion, or at least a friend, travelling with him, and both of them studied Jameson's badge, his worn and faded appearance and his tied-down sixgun as though he might also possess horns under his hat, and a tail.

The stage had a six-horse hitch. When it was a mile out of Sutherland the driver whistled up his animals, they hit their collars, the passengers were violently jarred, and the vehicle broke over into a rough, swift place.

Jameson braced his feet, crushed his hat down low and closed his eyes. The other passengers watched him with disbelief. He slept like a child, his body riding out the jolts and twists as though he were completely relaxed and comfortable.

They stopped three times. Twice the stops were to change hitches and the way-stations were isolated, but the third stop was a village called West Branch. It had been established by some sect or other, and the few settlers still acted as though enough misfortunes during the earlier days in this renegade and Apache-infested territory had pretty well weaned them away from too much rules and regulation.

West Branch has two saloons and one church. It also had a pool-hall, a card room, and what looked to Jameson who had never been here before, like a dancehall over the firehouse, upstairs in the same building.

The bohunk-passenger and his interpreter, or friend, or kinsman or whatever he was, left the stage at West Branch. The last Jameson saw of them they were standing outside one of the saloons and the man who spoke English was trying to explain to the bohunk the name of the town. The immigrant would repeat his version of West Branch in his native speech, then he would look incredulously at his friend, then roll his eyes around as though he were bewildered to find West Branch had log and adobe buildings and saloons instead of streets of gold and marble palaces.

The travelling dentist was amused. He and Jameson had the coach to themselves from here on. No fresh passengers got aboard at West Branch.

They got a new driver at West Branch. He was a little more considerate of his passengers than the previous whip had been, then in fact most coach-drivers were for that matter. As he loosened his lines north of town the hitch settled forward without a lunge. It picked up the pace gradually and by the time the stage was rocketing ahead at full speed both Jameson and the dentist who was so solicitous of his little valises, were prepared for the bumps and jolts.

Jameson slept again. The dentist eyed this accomplishment with green envy, clutched his valises and bleakly rode out the bucking and swaying wide awake and fully resigned. There was no other way for people to cover great distances if they would not, or could not, do it on horseback.

The final leg of the journey was made through accumulating late-day shadows, and over the last six- or eight-miles Jameson was awake. He and the dentist had eaten at a waystation about an hour and a half past high noon. They would be unable to buy another meal until they arrived in Clayton. Not that it mattered since they had both eaten like horses back at the way-station, but that much open and uninhabited country signified that north of the middle areas of Arizona territory there was a lot of privately-controlled cow-country.

"Good grass," opined the dentist, and because of the look he got from Jameson he smiled and also said, "I wasn't born pulling teeth. I'm like Doc Holliday in that respect-only in reverse. I rode the range for ten years before I studied dentistry and became a doctor of it. Doc was a dentist first, then an outlaw." The passenger chuckled. "I've been too busy working on teeth to become an outlaw yet." He winked. "But I'm only forty so I figure there's time yet." He leaned and pointed out where an immense plateau rose up out of the far-distant grassland. The plateau was totally flat on top and looked to be perhaps as much as fifty miles in depth.

Jameson, who had never seen that plateau before, said, "Probably called table rock. I've seen a lot of them and that's what they're usually called." He eyed the dentist; if the man were so impressed by that big flat-roofed mountain out there, he had to be a stranger to the territory because Arizona had a lot of plateaus just like that one. But Jameson refrained from making enquires. He instead rolled a smoke while leaning forward upon the edge of the plunging seat and managed it so expertly he did not lose a single flake of tobacco. That too impressed the dentist.

Dusk arrived while they were still boring ahead the long, wide distances. With shadows forming they eventually began to see cattle in little bunches here and there upon both sides of the road, and when the coachman slackened pace allowing his horses to walk in order to be able to deliver them dry and not winded at the corralyard in Clayton, Jameson risked a long look out the left side of the stage. He could make out nothing up ahead until the road made a light bend, then he was able to catch a glimpse of distant rooftops under a reddening sun.

He pulled back and said, "Another hour," and tipped down his hat, braced his feet and folded his arms. He did not sleep but he rested, and since he'd already had enough sleep the rest was just as beneficial.

They arrived upon the outskirts of Clayton slightly more than an hour later, with evening settling, with the main thoroughfare up through town completely devoid of pedestrians, and with the setting sun adding fresh hues to the storefronts and rooftops so that this old trading-post town which had been built largely of logs, hauled down from the distant mountains, looked decidedly picturesque in its broad grassland setting, with an occasional far butte visible miles out.

The stage company had its yard at the lower end of town, adjacent to a large liverybarn which seemed to also serve as a local freight depot. At least when the stage halted out front of its corralyard to allow all passengers to alight, Jameson saw several huge pole corrals where large, placid harness-horses and mules were quietly eating.

The dentist nodded to Jameson, grasped a valise under each arm and hiked briskly in the direction of the rooming-house. He had evidently been in Clayton before; that, or else he had a knack for locating rooming-houses.

A burly, balding man, weathered and scarred and seasoned-looking strolled forth from the stage office, looking steadily at Jameson. He had a star on his vest but even without it he would have looked as though he would be someone in authority.

"Marshal Clive Gentry," he told Jameson, and thrust forth a broad, thick hand. After the handshake he said, "As many miles as you've road on that contraption, Deputy, you ought to have a hell of a parched gullet. I'll stand the first round across the road."

Because this clearly was Town Marshal Gentry's way of buying enough privacy and enough time to get all the details of an affair which intrigued him, Jameson went along. He probably would have gone after a beer or two anyway because as a matter of fact his throat was parched.

The saloon was pleasantly fragrant from horse-sweat and tobacco-smoke. It had only one other occupied table, where some oldtimers were at a pinochle session, and probably because it was suppertime there were no other patrons lining the bar. They would undoubtedly arrive later.

The burly lawman got a pitcher and two glasses, guided Jameson to the table Gentry favored, and as they sat Gentry filled both glasses with beer from the pitcher. Then he smiled. "Damned long ride for you, Deputy. Damned serious trouble for the both of us if you don't have a hell of a good reason for getting me to hold Marshal Buck Whitney here in Clayton. He's mad as a wet hen."

"You've told him I was coming?" Jameson asked.

"No," stated the burly lawman, lifting his beer glass. "All I told him was that it wouldn't be humane for him to move his prisoner, Hollister being as sick as he is and all. I told him he was plumb free to catch the next stage out if he was of a mind to, and he got pretty mad at me. He refused to leave until he could haul his prisoners off with him." Gentry drank beer like most people drank water. He was reaching for the pitcher as he said, "It wasn't just Hollister being sick that made me decide to keep them here...care for a refill?" Lincoln Jameson shook his head no and Deputy Gentry continued, "It wasn't just the wire from you, neither. Whitney doesn't have any papers on the prisoners. You're supposed to have at least arrest warrants, and the story he told of the girl helping her father escape doesn't hold any sense. I tried to get the girl off to herself, but Hollister sticks close enough to those two people to be their shadows...Never had one like this before, Deputy...This is good beer. Don't you like beer, Deputy?"

Chapter **Twelve**

Jameson had no particular plans. Up until he had arrived in Clayton, he'd been occupied in either trying to recover from the personal exhaustion all this recent trouble had caused him, or else in seeking to catch up with either the Hollisters or Marshal Whitney. He'd had plenty of time on the stagecoach to formulate a plan of action-except that he had needed that time to sleep. Now, as he sat in the quiet saloon with Clayton's constable, marveling at Gentry's thirst, he decided that because he was less confident of his position with respect to Chuck Hollister, and because Hollister being ill would probably make it unnecessary for Jameson to do much about him for a few days in any case, he decided to concentrate for the time being upon Nellie Hollister.

He asked where the girl was. Gentry cocked a jaundiced eye. "She's pretty," he acknowledged, and continued to gaze at Jameson as though he had suspected this might be the deputy's approach all along. "Pretty, and she sure needs friends about now."

Jameson curbed his temper. "She's pretty" he agreed, "but since that don't have much to do with why I'm here suppose for now we just let that slide. Whitney had no warrant for her."

Gentry sat relaxed, comfortably awash with beer. "He told me federal officers aren't accountable to town marshals. He might be right for all I know. I never learned much book-law. But here in Clayton I'm the law and when I ask for warrants I figure on seeing them."

"He's got a Colorado warrant on Hollister," stated Jameson, "but he's got no warrant on the girl, and he don't have extradition papers on either one of them. On top of that, he took those people out of my jailhouse down in Ruby with no authority, which was illegal as all hell, and he's trying to get out of Arizona Territory and over to Colorado with them without extradition papers, which is also illegal as all hell."

Marshal Gentry smiled softly. "We used to have a doctor here in Clayton, he said, "but he died a few years back."

Because Jameson saw no connection between this and his former statement concerning extradition, he frowned and said, "What's that got to do with it?"

"I don't think Chuck Hollister is sick," stated Gentry, still loosely smiling. "At first I thought so, when he fell out of the stage and folks all rushed up to be helpful, and his daughter wrung her hands and cried and all...But you know, Deputy, a man in my business gets so he can sort of feel things. I got a hunch Marshal Whitney thinks the same as me. I don't believe Hollister is sick at all. Maybe a little sick-he looks soft and puny to me after all those years in prison-but he's not real sick. My guess is that him and his daughter cooked this up and when she opened the door of the coach over in front of the way-station, and he moaned then fell out upon the plank walk, grinding his teeth and groaning and sort of frothing at the mouth and all-I'm here to tell you even those yardmen from the stage company's backlot come charging out to help. Marshal Whitney got shouldered aside; folks picked Hollister up and packed him over to the hotel. A couple of them came for me at the jailhouse, but what the hell could I do? My business is jugging drunk cowboys and so forth. Anyway, I went over there, cleared out the room except for Hollister, his girl and the Marshal, and I'll tell you for a fact, Hollister sure looked sick...But couple of hours later when I was over there, Deputy, I commenced having my doubts...If we still had a doctor here..."

Jameson said, "I hope he isn't sick. But for the time being I want to get the girl turned loose. Later, we can worry about her pappy."

Marshal Gentry sat and studied the younger man wearing that deputy's badge. Gentry did not look like the kind of man to be impressed, not by a deputy sheriff and not by a deputy federal marshal, but his next comment suggested that this might be an incorrect assumption.

"How?" he said. "That man is a Deputy U.S. Marshal. How do you go about taking a prisoner away from a Deputy U.S. Marshal?"

"She's not a prisoner," exclaimed Jameson. "Where's the warrant?" He leaned to arise. "Show me where she is."

Gentry made no immediate move to arise. He skeptically eyed the deputy sheriff, his attitude seeming to be one of personal attachment, at least for the time being although it was hard to reconcile this attitude with the way he had been talking.

Then he arose and led the way out of the saloon, not speaking another word.

Night was close, Clayton's earlier appearance was now softened by a steadily increasing variety of nightfall, which for the time being lacked starlight in noticeable proportions. Down at the liverybarn there was a bright lantern throwing soft orange brilliance from mid-way down the runway out to the roadway, and at the general store someone had lighted a couple of lamps although the front door was closed with a sign to that effect in the window.

Across from the saloon where the pair of lawmen were, was a small, brightly lighted shop which Gentry said was the local harness work. "Always behind," he explained. "Works late every night and doesn't ever seem to catch up."

Jameson was not particularly interested. "Which is the hotel?" he asked, and Gentry gave him another of those dour, skeptical glances and turned as before, without speaking, to lead the way.

Clayton's hotel was a rooming-house of the same variety to be found in just about every cow-town, but if its proprietor preferred to call it a 'hotel' it was improbable that anyone around Clayton, or travelling through for that matter, cared in the slightest.

There were three men in the parlor when Gentry and Jameson entered. All three of them were armed, unsmiling, tough-looking individuals. They glanced at Gentry and past him at Jameson. No one nodded or spoke or smiled until Gentry said, "The fella from down south," and started past, then the three big solemn-faced men infinitesimally nodded. Jameson nodded back. Fifteen feet along the poorly lit corridor he tapped Gentry's arm.

"Friends of yours?"

Gentry nodded. "Local blacksmith and his two sons."

"You stationed them here?"

"In a mess like this," the lawman said, pausing before a corridor doorway, "we got a vigilante committee here in Clayton that jumps in and helps." Gentry raised a fist to knock and turned to glace at Jameson the same time. "By the way, Whitney isn't in here. It's just the little lady and her paw. Whitney is down at the jailhouse writing some reports to Denver and writing some telegraph messages he wants sent."

For the time being that explanation had to suffice. Gentry knocked, then spoke his name, and a moment later Nellie Hollister opened the door. She started to step way to allow Gentry to enter the room when she caught sight of Jameson farther back in the shadows. She seemed to suddenly become solid stone.

Gentry walked past jerking his thumb. "You'll know this fella, Miss," he said and continued on over to halt at the bedside gazing at the grey-faced man lying there.

Nellie Hollister shook her head in disbelief, then she said, "I'll never understand how you do it, Deputy. How you manage to show up where no one expects you."

He smiled at her. "It's easy to figure out. I lose a lot of sleep. How is your pappy?"

She leaned on the door and answered without taking her eyes off him. "Very ill. But of course you won't believe that, will you?"

He did not answer the question. He instead asked one of his own. "Do you still believe we're enemies?"

She finally closed the door behind him, slowly and thoughtfully. "It was so much of a coincidence, Deputy, you riding out of Ruby and staying away while Marshal Whitney conveniently came along and with a perfectly clear trail ahead, took us out of your jailhouse and out of your territory."

He stared, momentarily forgetting her father and Marshal Gentry. "You think that was pre-arranged?"

"It could not have worked better, Deputy."

He started to redden. "If I'd wanted to hand you over I didn't have to go through all that trouble." He turned, because his anger was increasing every second he remained over by the door looking at her.

The man in the bed eyed Jameson cautiously. "You sure covered a heap of ground," he said by way of greeting.

Jameson's anger was still strong enough to make him say, "Yeah; and you're still pulling tricks on folks. But I wouldn't have thought you could do it to Whitney."

"If you're ever in prison for twenty years, Deputy, you'll know how desperate a man can become the closer he gets to going back. But it wasn't all play-acting. I got sick all right. I've had trouble with my innards for years. Last few years these attacks been getting a little worse."

"But you could walk out of here and ride a coach back to Ruby," stated Jameson. "Mister Hollister, I got that warrant for you on the horse-stealing charge. You can go back with me or you can go north with Whitney, but you can't lie here forever, can you? No one's going to remain convinced you're sick next week or the week after."

Nellie came around to the far side of the bed and lightly rested her fingers atop her father's inert hand atop the covers. She looked from him across to Jameson. "Can you make it stick? Can you use that Arizona Territory warrant to supersede the one from Denver?"

Gentry, to whom this charge of horse-stealing was a fresh innovation, stood stroking his jaw and looking skeptically from one of them to the other

When Jameson said, "Nellie; this is still Arizona Territory. Our warrants take precedence here," Gentry gravely nodded his head, but when Jameson said, "Mister Hollister, you'd better make up your mind to make the trip back to Ruby on the next stage going south," Marshal Gentry began to darkly scowl.

He said, "Whoa, Deputy. By any chance are you figuring to sneak them out of Clayton on the morning coach south? You'd be leaving me with one hell of a mad federal officer."

Jameson had his answer-he thought. "Do you folks up around Clayton believe horse-theft is a serious crime, Marshal?"

"Of course. Everyone figures that, not just around Clayton, and I heard you say you got a warrant for this fella as a horse-thief. But I'd still have a mad federal marshal on my hands."

Jameson smiled a little. "He'd ought to be able to understand how something like this happens, Marshal. All I'd be doing is escorting a fella from the hotel to the way-station. I wouldn't be violating the law by taking him out of your jailhouse, would I? As for the young lady…"

"Yeah; no warrant," muttered Gentry and turned to the far-wall window where he leaned a little to glance down the dark roadway southward where a light burned brightly in his jailhouse office.

Moments later as he straightened around he said, "He sure as hell will come after you, Deputy."

Jameson's answer was matter-of-factly given. "I guess that would be his right."

Gentry had not made that observation because he cared what the answer from Jameson would be, he had said it to clarify in his own mind something which appealed strongly to him.

"That'll get the whole lot of you out of my bailiwick, Deputy, including Marshal Whitney." He stepped to the foot of the bed. "Can you walk, Mister Hollister?"

The ill man said, "Yes, I can walk. But Marshal Gentry, being hanged as a horse-thief in Arizona don't strike me as being a lot better than being re-sentenced in Colorado. Up there, they'll double the time I still have to serve, but they won't hang me."

Jameson butted in. "That damned warrant I hold for you isn't signed. Murray Foster, the liveryman you stole those two horses from when you were trying to escape from Whitney, refused to sign it."

Hollister considered Jameson's look of exasperation for a moment, then said, "He won't change his mind?"

"No. He thinks Nellie stole the horses and he refused to prosecute her. He said she was too young and pretty, or something like that."

"But she didn't..."

Gantry came back into the discussion with a question for Jameson. "How can you haul these folks out of here on a warrant which is supposed to take precedence over the federal warrant, if your warrant isn't signed?"

Jameson's color started to come up again but the light was too poor in the room for others to notice. "It's still a warrant for Hollister's arrest," he replied, then briefly held his breath because he was not sure this bluff would work. "That fella down at Ruby could still change his mind and sign it, Mister Gentry."

Clayton's town marshal continued to stand stroking his jaw, but after a while he shifted position a little, at the foot of the bed and said, "I wish to hell you folks were out of here."

"What are the chances of hiring a special stage so we can get out of here?" Jameson asked.

This suggestion seemed to take Gentry by total surprise, which lasted only a moment before he suddenly smiled expansively, the first wide smile Jameson had seen on the marshal's face since arriving in Clayton.

"Cost you fifty-dollars," he exclaimed. "Including the coach, four-up hitch and the driver. Payable in advance." He held out his hand. "That's my business. I've owned the local franchise for six years. You got fifty-dollars, Deputy?"

Jameson dug deep for the packet of greenbacks in his trouser pocket but before he could count the cash to determine how much he actually was carrying, Nellie Hollister handed Marshal Gentry six folded-flat greenbacks which were still warm from within her bodice where she had been carrying them.

Gentry was unmindful of the money's warmth, he was only mindful that it was the correct amount, and afterwards Jameson was struck by the abrupt transformation. From a lawman who had been skeptical and who had been dragging his feet, to this suddenly brisk and business-like individual, the change had only required a few seconds.

It was amazing what a few folded greenbacks could do. Jameson dryly said, "Suppose Marshal Whitney hears about a special coach heading out of Clayton?"

"No one is going to inform him," stated Gentry, bringing forth a big leather wallet to stow the greenbacks safely into.

"Suppose he accuses you of complicity?" asked Jameson, and this time he got a dark scowl.

"Of what?"

"Complicity; of helping us head back south."

"Remember what I told you back over at the saloon, Deputy? I run the law in Clayton. Don't know one else run it. Least of all no outside lawmen, no matter who they are." Gentry turned towards Chuck Hollister. "Get out of there and let's get down to the corralyard!"

Chapter Thirteen

Hollister could walk but he was not very steady at it, nor was Jameson as convinced as Gentry was, that Chuck Hollister was pretending. Jameson's main reason for believing the fugitive was genuinely ill was because Nellie allowed her father to lean on her, and she was in other ways solicitous over his welfare. Jameson did not believe

Nellie Hollister was deceitful, not even though she had once come up behind him with a sixgun in her hand.

It was dark and when they entered the way-station room where Gentry told them to wait, there was a faint nip to the night, noticeable, but hardly more than noticeable.

Jameson left Hollister inside and went out back where Gentry was routing out some yardmen from their back-wall bunkhouse. There were two stages neatly parked, and in stalls adjacent to the bunkhouse, also along the rear log wall of the yard, were harness-horses.

Jameson, who'd had no inkling that Marshal Gentry was anything more than just another town constable, watched as Gentry gave orders which stage was to be hitched up, and decided that perhaps the uniquely detached attitude which he had noticed when he and Gentry had been over at the saloon, might have sprung from the fact that Gentry had more on his mind than simply a deputy sheriff with a federal deputy marshal, and a pair of unwanted fugitives.

One thing he was certain of: Gentry was a man whose motivations were just about as commercial as they could safely get.

The Clayton lawman came over where Jameson was standing and said, "Deputy; I'm going down to the jailhouse. When this coach is ready the driver will let you know. Get those folks on board and get the hell south of here as fast as you can and please don't come back." He offered a hand, which Jameson pumped and released, then Gentry turned without another glance and went briskly walking out of the yard and southward.

Jameson wagged his head. In his pursuit of the Hollisters he had been through his share of adventures, but this was the most intriguing one of them all. A town marshal who owned the stage franchise accepting money to get some fugitives out of his territory.

Jameson returned to the dark waiting-room where the Hollisters were. Nellie looked even younger in the pale starlight, and her father looked more actually ill.

Jameson rolled a smoke, explained what Gentry had said and what he was probably doing down at his jailhouse-keeping the federal officer down there until the stage pulled out of town-and he dropped down besides Chuck Hollister with a sigh.

"If we make it back down to Ruby," he said, "we'll still have problems." He glanced at Hollister. "Outsmarting Whitney isn't the same as getting away scot free. He'll get extradition papers for you eventually, then he'll come back and do it legal next time."

Nellie leaned to say, "Does my father have to sit down there and wait, Deputy? If you've gone to all this trouble to get us away from Whitney, and you don't have legal warrants for us-aren't you helping an outlaw and doesn't that mean you can also be in trouble? I was wondering-couldn't we still get over the line into Mexico?"

Jameson had not really thought this entire situation through to a logical conclusion, but he knew one thing which he would not do that was take the easy way out; he would not simply allow the Hollisters to go over the line. Not because Whitney would then be after him for aiding and abetting, but because he remained convinced that Chuck Hollister deserved more than he was getting.

Fortunately, he was not required to answer Nellie Hollister's question. The gaunt, high-cheekboned stage driver with his droopy mustache making him look more cadaverous than ever, appeared in the rear doorway to announce that the stage was ready to roll.

Outside, in the corral yard a pair of disconsolate-looking individuals were standing near the lead horses looking at the people crossing from the dark waiting-room. Not a word was said. When the passengers were inside, the door closed after them, the hostlers stepped clear, the driver whistled softly and moved his hitch dead ahead out into the empty roadway-then he did a peculiar thing, instead of turning southward down through town past the stores and the jailhouse, he turned northward and left Clayton by the upper environs. Once clear, he swung westerly until he was well away from the backlots, then he finally lined his hitch out southward and let the horses walk all the way to the lower, southerly end of Clayton where he angled around and got back up on the roadway.

Chuck Hollister and Lincoln Jameson exchanged a look. Clearly, since the driver had probably not done all that on his own initiative, he had been instructed to do it, and for only one apparent reason, so that no stagecoach would go rattling down the main roadway, back in town, past the jailhouse where Marshal Whitney would surely have sprang to his feet to ascertain what was happening.

Neither Jameson nor Hollister mentioned what was uppermost in both their minds, but when they were safely back upon the southward run and making fair time Hollister smiled at his daughter.

Jameson lit a smoke. They had a full night of riding ahead of them. There might be two or three stops, but even so they would be together for a very long while. He said, "Mister Hollister, about that bank-clerk you say shot the banker and killed him when you raided that bank...There had to be some information about him somewhere, maybe in the files of the bank, but somewhere."

Hollister shrugged. "In twenty years, nothing was ever turned up."

"Did anyone ever make a real search?" asked Jameson and got an answer he did not expect.

"I looked," exclaimed Nellie Hollister. "I wrote letters, made inquires, even tried to find his family or some of his friends...Deputy, you may not believe this, but that man might just as well have disappeared off the face of the earth...Once, I talked to a man who thought he might have met the bank clerk out in California. When I wrote out there, they had no record of any such a person."

Chuck Hollister ruefully said, "You would hardly figure that a fella who accidently killed someone would get so afraid over it they'd change their name and go into hiding just like it was a deliberate murder, would you?"

Jameson let the question go unanswered. He said, "Nellie, when you were doing all your digging, did you happen to go to the law and see if there was any way to get a re-trial?"

She had done this, among other things. "I don't believe I left many stones unturned, Deputy. As for retrial-the judge in Denver who sentenced my father was the brother of the banker who was supposedly killed by my father."

Jameson stared at her. "His brother?" He paused a moment then said, "Well hell; there should have been a disqualification!"

She showed Jameson a winterly smile. "I'd heard it said, Mister Jameson, there that we have two kinds of law in this country. I was never convinced that was true. But after my father was brought to trial, I knew it was true. The judge refused to disqualify himself and the court-appointed lawyer who defended my father said it didn't matter. He said my father was lucky to get off alive."

She waited a moment, felt for her father's hand and clenched it, then also said, "Mister Jameson, I believed that myself; I thanked God they didn't sentence my father to death. I'm sure that must have been in the judge's mind right up until it became apparent that my father could not have fired the shot which killed the banker."

Jameson expelled a big breath, slowly looked from the daughter to the father, then continued to let his gaze roam until it went beyond the coach out into the darkness on all sides of the stagecoach.

Later, he slept, and when he awakened with a slight ache in the back both the Hollisters were watching him owlishly, and when they saw that his eyes were open the fugitive said, "If Whitney goes before that same judge and tells his story of what happened down here in Arizona Territory, they'll also issue a warrant for you, I'm sure of that."

Jameson hid a yawn then scratched. "It takes forever. Colorado is a state. Arizona is a territory. States are governed by civilian residents who vote on everything, Territories are governed by the military. It takes forever for the military to recognize a demand put upon it by civilians. I've seen this work. Anyway-the more I learn about this mess, Mister Hollister, the more it smells bad to me. Maybe, when we can get back to Ruby, what you folks had ought to do is find an attorney here in the Territory who would be willing to file for an appeal and a new trial."

Nellie said, "Deputy, that money I gave Marshal Gentry was half of all my savings I have in this world. Do you know any lawyers who work for nothing?"

The driver slackened off, the coach rocked down to a gradual halt, and Jameson climbed out to look enquiringly around. They were on flat ground without a tree or butte or a building in sight, but there was a stone trough besides the road and as the driver swarmed down he said, "Buckets are in the boot, if you'd care to lend a hand, Mister."

They watered the horses, stood a while in the cooling night smoking and allowing the horses to blow a little, to stamp their feet and rest.

The driver was a taciturn man. Each time Jameson attempted to strike up a conversation the driver would grunt and stand there, arms folded, like a cigar-store Indian, so Jameson gave it up.

Later, when they were on the way again Chuck Hollister slept fitfully and during one of those interludes his daughter confided in Deputy Jameson that it wasn't his stomach which had made the trouble back at Clayton, and that it had not been play-acting as everyone had seemed to eventually believe.

"He's had heart trouble all his adult life. They told him in prison he wouldn't live to see fifty."

Jameson almost said they had been wrong; as the words were formed it suddenly struck him that he could be very wrong. Cautiously, he said, "How old is your father?"

"Fifty-eight."

Jameson rummaged for his tobacco and papers.

The night seemed almost endless. Jameson was less sleepy than his companions, evidently. He watched them both fall asleep, waken and drop off again. Long before he felt the coach slackening and the driver letting up as his horses picked out an easy gait to follow, he guessed about where they were and tried several times despite the darkness to pick out landmarks.

Finally, when they passed a broad site at the eastern edge of the coach-road and Jameson picked up the scent of wood-smoke and coals, he knew where they were. There had always been a lay-by six miles above Ruby on the east side where freighters went into camp on their way into town as well as on their way out of town. They were already beyond that place when Jameson leaned out to look, but the smells were strong and unmistakable.

He was punching his hat back into shape from the last time he'd attempted to look out and had hit the upper half of the door with the upper half of his head, when Nellie Hollister smiled at him.

He was sheepish. "You never quite manage it and I'd ought to know; I've been getting hit in the head like that since I was big enough to ride a stage and poke my head out."

Her answer brought the discussion of bumped heads and crushed hat-crowns to a close then and there. "I wasn't smiling over that, Mister Jameson. I was smiling at you. I don't think my father and I would have even made it down into Mexico, and I don't think we'd have managed at all, without your help. I owe you an apology."

He dropped the reshaped hat upon the back of his head and grinned back at her. "For what? It'd be a spoilt week if I didn't have some pretty young schoolteacher poke a gun in my face and take a prisoner out of my jail-or at least try to do that."

She said, "Mister Jameson, are you married?"

That was too abrupt a switch even for Jameson. He blinked owlishly at her, and from beside her where they had both thought he had been asleep her father drowsily said, "He's not married yet, Nellie, but he's well spoken for. Mrs. West told me that day she acted as the jailer."

The driver whistled a high, keening call and his horses dropped to a steady walk. They were upon the outskirts of town. He had been jogging for the past few miles, which meant that the chain tugs had been rattling incessantly and loudly. Now, as everything went slack and the racket stopped, Jameson could hear the late-night silence for the first time in six miles.

The driver leaned, expectorated, then leaned a little more and called down. "Ruby folks. I'll put in at the corral yard and you can get out down there."

The town was as still as a cemetery, and although the log gates of the corral yard were open, there were no lights anywhere in Pete Clifford's compound. No one had expected this coach, and even if they had it was improbable that they would have remained up and stirring until it arrived. Caring for his horses would be the driver's responsibility, the same as parking his rig out of the way would be.

When he tooled up into the yard and cut a wide angle to turn with the coach facing the gate but to one side, where it could be hitched up handily and driven directly out again, the driver hit is rear binders, flung his lines to one side and climbed off the high seat hand over hand.

Jameson piled out first. There was a nip in the air. He stood aside holding the coach door until Hollister and his girl were out too, then he motioned for them to walk ahead. He herded them down to his jailhouse, herded them inside and after lighting a lamp, he finally herded them down to the same cells they had formerly occupied. He hung the lamp from a wall-peg and caught Nellie's funny little humorous smile as she walked past into the cell. He grinned at her.

"If you're hungry I'll go rout Leslie out, Nellie."

She faced him fully. "Get some rest, Deputy. We'll make out very well until morning. That will only be a couple of hours anyway, won't it?"

He left them, went up and barred the cell-room door, yawned mightily, pitched aside his hat and sank down at the chair behind the desk, cocked both booted feet atop the old desk and leaned back.

Nellie had been right; he deserved some rest. What she had failed to consider, probably because she was less seasoned and less skeptical in matters of this kind than Jameson was, the possibility that Deputy U.S. Marshal

Buck Whitney, who was also very wise and knowledgeable in this kind of an affair, might just have somehow or other discovered what Jameson had done, and be on his way through the night towards Ruby, to make another attempt at abducting those people in the cell-room.

It was not too probable, but it was not quite impossible either. Jameson had not gone through all he had survived the past day and night just to have it all wiped out because in the last lap he had let his guard down a little.

Chapter Fourteen

Morning arrived with no sign of Deputy U.S. Marshal Buck Whitney, so if he were on the way he had not as yet got back down into the country.

But Jameson had another set of visitors. Old Man McCallister from the north-westernly cow-country arrived with a dead Mexican tied across a horse and had an outsized sense of indignation. What he did not know was, who the gringo was who had led those *Rurales* practically into his camp.

He met Jameson on the deputy's return from shaving and cleaning up; Jameson had been on his way to the café when that bleak old rancher and his equally as worn and unshaven and grim band of riders entered town up north and walked their horses with great deliberation all the way down to the jailhouse where they tied up and swung off. What few people were abroad, mostly storekeepers on their way to unlock their places of business, saw the range riders, the dead *Rurale* and Old Man McCallister, and were properly impressed. Jameson certainly was; he crossed over from in front of the café to look at the *Rurale*. Old Man McCallister said, "That's only one of them. There was maybe eight or ten more, but it was dark as the inside of a boot and they hit us so sudden we scarcely had time to get out and protect the remuda before they tried to fight clear and get away...Some son of a bitch they were chasing, a gringo from hereabouts, led those devil riders over there and led them into a fight with us so he could scamper away. I figure he was probably a horse-thief; maybe he was after our remuda too, and maybe he was even leading those Mexicans, but I tell you for a fact, Deputy, I'd give five good horses to lay my eyes on him for what he done-leading them Mexicans right up almost into our camp and using us like that."

Jameson, who had already made up his mind to ride back out there and explain all that had happened, and tell the range men how grateful he was for their inadvertent aid, gazed upon the bitter-eyed and ferocious old cowman and decided this was not the time; decided in fact that maybe the right time might never arrive.

He said, "Any of your crew injured?"

"No," exclaimed the old man, "but that was only because I never hired riders who couldn't shoot straight and ride hard."

"What happened to the Mexicans?"

"Happened?" exclaimed the old cowman. "I'll tell you what happened to them mangy bastards, they run ahead of us for maybe three miles heading for the border. This here one-we didn't even know we'd killed him until, on the way back, we found this horse standing beside a dead Mexican." McCallister looked at his tough-faced riding crew and jerked his head. "Might as well get breakfast since we're in town. Sam will take the horses down to Murray Foster's and tell him if he don't have them cuffed and grained and stalled and hayed by the time we come for them, we'll slit his ears and pull both arms through them."

Jameson said nothing as the range men handed their reins to the youngest cowboy then followed McCallister across the road. After they had all departed including the youth with the saddle stock, Jameson was left with a dead Mexican belly-down across his saddle, and a worn-down Mexican horse. He untied the beast and led it around behind his jailhouse where there was a dilapidated old carriage or wagon shed. He placed the

Rurale on a trestle-table in the shed which was used for exactly this purpose, emptied the dead man's pockets for whatever he could find which might make notification of next of kin possible, then took the Mexican horse down the back-alley, and because Murray was busy up front with the horses, Jameson unsaddled the Mexican horse, washed his back, corralled him and fed him before returning to his jailhouse.

He was hungry. More than that, he was in the mood for a cup of Leslie West's superb coffee. But right now, he did not want to share the bench over there with those disgruntled range men.

He went into the cell-room to tell the Hollisters what had happened, and to explain about those other *Rurales,* the ones which had got away plus the other two or three which had stolen some stage company horses in order to get Jameson out of town, and when Chuck Hollister began to wag his head Jameson said, "Whitney has got one hell of a reputation, so I've been told. From now on I'll be an authority about that." He agreed to get their breakfast as soon as McCallister's range riders left town, and went up front.

Among the dead Mexican's personal property Jameson discovered a soiled scrap of paper which, when it had been unraveled and flattened out, turned out to contain Whitney's instructions to the *Rurales* leader. It did not mention Jameson. In fact, it had not been written to cover the most serious aspect of the Mexican involvement, it had instead been written to define what Whitney expected the *Rurales* to do about stopping Hollister at the border. It specifically mentioned seeing to it that the *Rurales* got the entire reward for the escape.

Jameson put the piece of paper to one side and picked up what seemed to be a letter, but since it was written in Spanish he put it aside; his knowledge of Spanish was limited to speaking border-country, cow-range Mexican, which was only sketchily related to correct Spanish, and he could not read Spanish at all, correct or any variety of the language. He was confidant however, from studying the letter that it contained both the name of the defunct *Rurale* and what had to be the address of someone who had written the letter, and which Jameson assumed would be a relative, or at least a close friend, someone to whom Jameson could write about the Mexican's passing.

He would not write to the next-of-kin, though, with any hope that they might get up to Ruby in time to claim the body. Summer was coming; he had no intention of allowing his trestle-table out in the wagon-shed to be occupied more than a day or two by that Mexican out there.

There was a Baptist preacher in town, and as soon as he could be contacted to say a few words over the grave, and as soon as the diggers could be induced to make the hole in the ground, that dead *Rurale* was going to be permanently planted.

McCallister eventually left town at a stiff-legged jog with his hard-looking riding-crew. Jameson went to the café for a belated breakfast and for the tray of food for the Hollisters. Leslie insisted on knowing in detail exactly what had happened since the Hollisters had been sprinted away, and since Jameson had got them back and returned to town with them. He told her between mouthfuls all that he thought she had to know. If he had detailed the entire story he would have been sitting there at her counter until high noon.

When he finished he looked her in the eyes and said, "Old Man McCallister needs a woman at his ranch. Someone whose cooking and care would improve the old devil's disposition."

She looked nonplussed, but only temporarily, then she hauled herself up very erect and said, "Just what do you think you are doing-trading horses or something? I wouldn't go out there if Mister McCallister proposed to me himself, in person, and promised me the moon."

"But you don't figure to stay single," Jameson told her. "I heard that on good authority."

She scoffed. "What authority! You're just making this all up and you know it."

"No I'm not. Mister Hollister told me on the ride back from Clayton that you had your sights set on someone around here."

She stood a moment returning his gaze, then very slowly she started to redden. Her eyes did not turn aside though until he shoved back his plate and reached for the coffee cup, and said, "If you wouldn't hitch double with McCallister, who would you climb into double-harness with?"

She looked at his bare plate and leaned in to take it. She hovered upon the verge of turning and retreating to her cooking area, face pleasantly pink and her eyes fixed upon the empty plate in her hands. She was clearly struggling with herself; was clearly trying to come to grips with an answer to his question.

He finally said, "Leslie, you ought to go down to the jailhouse and cheer up Nellie. She's a woman and she doesn't have any friends...."

"Woman my ass!" exclaimed Leslie. "She's just a girl! There's a huge difference between women and girls....are you seriously considering....Lincoln Jameson!...Do you know how old she is?"

He knew. "Twenty-one."

"And you turned thirty-five this last spring!"

He had no idea she knew how old he was, to the year, nor when his birthday was.

"You are almost fifteen years older than that girl, Lincoln Jameson! Almost old enough to be her father!"

He pondered that briefly, and meanwhile Leslie had one more comment to make.

"Do you think a man like you could be happy with a girl like her? I can tell you right now, mister, you couldn't be."

He fished around for his tobacco sack. "She asked me if I was single." He looked at the paper trough in his hands as he worked up the cigarette.

She ignored that to say, "You need more than a pretty face. I've known you for years. I've watched you, and if ever there was a man who needed a woman, you're it Lincoln!"

Her face turned red, then she said, "Lincoln?"

He lighted up and raised his eyes. "Yes, Leslie."

"Are you ready?"

"Ready for what?"

"To get married," she asked.

She was standing erect, hands on her hips, the way she usually stood when she was dead serious about something. She was a full woman in every way that a man expected a woman to be.

He was indeed ready. He'd been ready for some time now, but he'd been less fearful of rejection from her, than he was ready to abandon his single status which, for all its clear and patent drawbacks, had its advantages too.

He cleared his throat and considered the ash upon the tip of the cigarette. In a low tone he said, "You and I?"

"Yes."

He looked up. "I'm ready. Are you ready?"

She barely got to say "Yes," when the door opened and Pete Clifford barged in as dour in the face as always. He ignored Leslie and shoved out a fist containing a letter addressed to Deputy Sheriff Lincoln Jameson at Ruby, Arizona Territory.

Clifford shot Leslie a glance and dropped down at the counter. "Whatever you got," he said by way of ordering a meal, "as long as some of your fresh coffee goes with it." When she stood like a statue looking steadily at the deputy, Pete's dark brow darkened still more. "You going deaf, Leslie?" he growled, and Jameson raised his eyes from the letter to say, "Is that how your folks taught you to address a lady?"

Clifford blinked. "I only said...Hey, what's the matter with the two of you?"

Leslie whirled around and ran into her cooking-area and Jameson glared as he arose, clenching the letter. "If you hadn't brought me something that makes my whole damned day, I think I'd punch you in the nose!"

Clifford twisted almost completely around as he watched Jameson stride out of the café and across the sun-bright roadway. Then he faced and peered down in the direction of the curtain with those big blue flowers on it, and decided that something had happened in the café just prior to his arrival, and for the time being, until he knew what it was, his wisest course would be to mind his own business, eat his breakfast in silence, and get the hell out of the café as soon as possible.

It wasn't a bad surmise at that.

Jameson took the letter Pete Clifford had given him to his office where he re-read it, then he marched down into the cell-room letter in hand, but Nellie did not give him a chance to open his mouth. She fretfully said, "We're beholden to you, Mister Jameson, but I don't think that entitles you to starve us. Where is the tray?"

He didn't have it. In fact neither he nor Leslie West had mentioned the prisoners this morning. With a flourish he produced the cell-door key, wordlessly unlocked both doors and flung them wide.

"Go across and get your own breakfast," he told then, then faced her father in the opposite cell. "How are you feeling this morning, Mister Hollister?"

The fugitive, sitting disconsolately upon the edge of his wall-bunk, made a contrite smile and said, "I'll make it, Deputy."

Jameson entered the cell and raised the letter as he said, "Listen to this. First, I got to explain that when I first knew you were in the country I wrote the authorities up in Durango for a flyer and whatever else they had on you. This here is their answer." Jameson rattled the page in his hand.

"It says- concerning your enquiries about Chuck Hollister who walked away from a work detail last month, please be advised that we here at the penitentiary have been informed by the authorities in Denver that they are in receipt of a letter from the daughter of a man who recently died in San Francisco, which enclosed a confession that her father, the recently-deceased man, had accidentally shot and killed the banker who died during the commission of Chuck Hollister's bank robbery twenty-five years ago. We would therefore advise you, Deputy Jameson, if he is within your jurisdiction, that pending a complete legal review we have been instructed by the authorities in Denver not to do anything which may jeopardize his life, such as inaugurating a manhunt for him, and that he is at liberty to remain free until such time as formal ratification from Denver arrives absolving Hollister from having to serve any further time in the penitentiary."

Jameson lowered the paper and met the gaze of the man on the cot. Then he smiled and offered Hollister the letter. "Go across the café and read it for yourself over some decent coffee."

Nellie ran up and kissed Jameson on the cheek, then turned to extend both hands to her father. Hollister arose, clutching the letter as though it were his reprieve- which it evidently was. "That," he said to Jameson, "is the one thing I've always hoped might happen. That someday when his conscious wouldn't let him live with any longer, he'd come forward."

Jameson escorted them to the front office. He said nothing as he held the roadside door for them, but he was thinking that the bank clerk's conscious had to have been a lot punier than a lot of human consciences to have allowed the bank clerk to go right up to his death-bed before writing that letter.

On the other hand it was understandable that someone who had allowed the secret crime to go unrequited for so many years could not bring himself to confess any earlier because then he would have had to explain why he had not come forward years earlier.

In any case, as Jameson stood in the doorway watching the Hollisters cross Ruby's main roadway, arm in arm, free people, he felt as good as he had ever felt about his work and how he conducted himself lately. But in the back of his mind was the thundering black cloud of reckoning that was on its way to Ruby-a pissed off fella by the name of Deputy U.S. Marshal Buck Whitney.

Chapter Fifteen

Chuck Hollister and his daughter got a room at the boarding-house. Nellie brought that letter from Durango back to Jameson, and after handing it over she stood looking steadily at the deputy, and finally she sighed, turned her heel and departed.

Jameson put that letter and the note from Whitney to the dead *Rurale* in his pocket and went across to the café for another cup of coffee.

Outside the jailhouse he met the Baptist preacher on his way down to Murray's place and explained about the dead Mexican. The minister agreed to conduct services over the man. He also said he'd look up the town grave-diggers-who also worked as part-time hostlers for Murray Foster-and send them out to the cemetery.

Jameson made it across the road to the front of the café when Henry Cooper from the general store caught up to him. Henry looked quizzically at the deputy sheriff. "What the hell is all this fracas been going on around town for the past week-you lock up folks, someone taking them out of the jailhouse, and now you are fetching them back?"

It was not a story which could be detailed while two men stood outside the café in the pleasant morning sunlight. Jameson slapped the storekeeper on the shoulder as he started to turn away. "One of these days when we've both got plenty of time, I'll explain it."

"People around town are starting to talk," Henry Cooper bragged. "One of these days your shenanigans are going to catch up to you."

Jameson left Cooper standing there still looking quizzically and entered the café. Leslie smiled at him as though they hadn't been involved in a private disturbance some time earlier. She went once to get his coffee while he stepped over the counter-bench and sat down.

He was thinking back to that steak-dinner he'd abandoned while previously sitting in this exact spot, when one of the corral yard hostlers walked in, unshaven, unwashed, smelling strongly of horses and manure, and dropped down, looked over and said, "I'm going to quit that lousy stage company; they work your ass off and the pay isn't much better then riding the range. All hours of the night and day-now there's a coach arriving from up north, way over schedule, and I'm supposed to be there when it arrives even if I haven't had no breakfast yet."

Jameson started to be sympathetic. "I know it's a hard way to make a living. But there could be a foot of snow on the ground and it could be the middle of winter somewhere else-up north maybe-and you'd be a hell of a lot more miserable." He paused and looked steadily at the hostler. "What stage? The south-bound isn't due again until this evening."

The irritating hostler shrugged. "I don't know. We have been handling a lot of light freight lately. Maybe one of them freight stages."

Leslie appeared, smiled at Jameson and went down to ask the hostler what he wanted to eat. Behind her,

Jameson finished his coffee, carefully put a coin beside it, and leaned to arise.

Leslie turned with the hostler's order and threw a questioning look at the deputy. "You're coming back?" she asked and seemed inordinately interested in his reply. He smiled at her. "I've always come back. Sure; in about an hour maybe."

They stood looking at one another while the ravenous hostler wolfed down his breakfast with no concern in anything else around him.

His boss would have been interested in the way Leslie and Jameson were looking at one another, but his boss was not present.

Jameson said, "I don't recollect whether there's a moon or not, but these have been right nice nights for buggy-rising lately."

Leslie did not smile. "I close up about six."

He smiled at her. "Keep the coffee hot. I'll be back directly, and we can discuss it." He winked at her and walked out of the café.

The hostler finally raised his head. "Could I get more coffee Miss?"

Leslie turned without looking at the man and went back into her cooking area, while out front of the café Jameson paused to roll and light a smoke, then he strolled over to the way-station and was met in the corral yard gateway by Pete Clifford, the unsmiling local stage company supervisor. Pete said, "Beautiful day," and accompanied this remark with a look out and around.

Jameson agreed. "Nice day, for a fact. What is this stage that's due in directly?"

Clifford shrugged. "You know as much as I do. Couple fellas brought me a message saying there was an unscheduled coach coming and all they could say was that it was travelling light...Maybe it's a freight hauling coach. We're getting more and more into light freight these days. Aren't enough passengers coming this far south anymore; at least not over through Ruby." Clifford dug out a plug of tobacco from a shirt-pocket and whittled off a corner and pouched it. As he was replacing the chewing tobacco to his pocket he leaned a little to look up the roadway. "Maybe it's another of those chartered stages like came in after midnight last night."

Jameson nodded solemnly. "That's what I've been thinking about, Pete, and if it is, I want to be right here when it comes into sight."

A yardman came forward to ask Clifford's advice about something and Pete turned to go back deeper into the yard with the man leaving Jameson up there in the pleasant warmth of morning sunlight, smoking and casually studying the far northward stage-road, which was empty as far as a man could see, and was probably also empty farther than that because there was not even any dust from farther off.

The hostler from the café came rambling along, threw a nod at Jameson and sauntered into the yard sucking his teeth. Evidently, he felt differently now that he had been fed.

Over at the cantina that fish-eyed barman who had been imported to mind the place part of the time, came forth wearing his work-a-day apron, carrying a slop-bucket, and after looking left and right hurled the dirty water out into the roadway. This served a dual purpose; it got rid of the wash-water and it also settled any dust which was lying out front of the saloon beyond the tie-rack.

It was much too early for the saloon to have customers, but they always opened up as early as any other of the local merchants. In lieu of customers, they washed down and cleaned up over there so that, later in the day when customers began trickling in, the place would at least be presentable.

Jameson smoked, slouched over there in the corral yard gateway, watched the town come leisurely to life, watched people he had known, and had for the most part liked, for so many years, pick up where they had left off the night before, and when he saw the Hollisters outside on the shaded front veranda of the rooming-house, he thought they looked as though they also belonged.

Then someone whistled from back along the rear-wall of the corral yard, and Jameson dropped his smoke and leaned to look. Sure enough that spotter back there was correct, there was a dusty old coach in sight coming steadily southward at a loose lope.

Jameson sighed. The coach had the same worn, faded colors as that chartered coach he and the Hollisters had reached Ruby in the night before. That damned town marshal up at Clayton had not just got rid of all those troublemakers who had been arriving in his town lately, but he'd made a cool one hundred dollars while doing it.

Jameson turned, sauntered deeper into the yard, yanked loose the tie-down on his holstered colt, tipped down his hat brim so sunlight would not interfere, and by the time he could hear the oncoming coach he was ready.

Maybe his guess was wrong. Maybe it wasn't wrong. In either case he was ready, and he was willing.

The coach slackened pace out front and cut wide to roll directly up into the yard without stopping out front as was customary to disgorge passengers. This also aroused Jameson's suspicious.

Pete Clifford, who had retreated to his office some time before, now appeared in the doorway in the back-wall of the roadside office and leaned to watch the arrival of the chartered coach. His interest was cursory, evidently; his company got paid regardless of what the purpose of the strange stagecoach was in reaching the Ruby corral yard. He was accustomed to receiving and servicing chartered stages. The only time Clifford's settled expression of very mild interest changed was when he saw Jameson out there with the tie-down on his sixgun hanging loose and saw the way Jameson was standing. Then, Pete Clifford took a greater interest, but by then the stage was turning up into his yard.

Jameson did not recognize the driver. He would probably not have known the man in any case. Nor did it matter. He glanced up, saw the man sweep him with a moving glance as he pulled down his hitch, and as the driver kicked on his rear binders the coach's nearside door opened and Deputy U.S. Marshal Whitney sprang out looking rumpled and unshaven and cold-eyed.

Jameson did not give Whitney a chance. He drew and aimed the Colt as he called over to catch Whitney's attention. "Stand right where you are, Marshal!"

Whitney did not act entirely surprised. He too, had pulled loose the tie-down thong so that his Colt handle was readily accessible. He glared. There was no mistaking the clear fact that Buck Whitney was in an icy rage.

"Shed the gun," ordered Jameson. "You damned fool-you should have known I'd be waiting. Shed it!"

Whitney made no move to obey. "You think you can shoot down a federal peace officer and get way with it, go ahead and shoot," he snarled. "Jameson; I got three warrants. One for each of the Hollisters and one for you."

Jameson was not impressed. "Anyone can swear out a warrant and anyone can sign one. I'll tell you one more time, Marshal. Shed that gun. Otherwise I'm going to try and shoot it off your hip and I'm not a very good shot with handguns."

Jameson took slow aim. Whitney waited until the very last moment, then he reached slowly, lifted out the sixgun and dropped it into the dirt and dust.

Jameson walked closer, fished in a pocket, brought forth that crumpled paper he'd taken from the dead *Rurale*, and offered it. "Your handwriting," he asserted, "Take it and read it, Whitney. I took it off the carcass of a dead Mexican. I'm going to mail it to the U.S. Marshal up at Denver. He'd ought to know how one of his lousy deputies tries to bushwhack fugitives-using paid murderers."

Whitney read the paper, looked from it to Jameson then re-read the note before balling it up and tossing it to the ground. He sneered. "My job is to catch them. The U.S. Marshal said that himself. Go ahead and send that note to him. Even if he doesn't like the idea he probably won't do much."

Jameson fished forth the other paper, the one from the authorities up at Durango. He offered that paper too, and when Whitney seemed reluctant, Jameson cocked the gun in his hand.

Whitney took the letter, opened it and read it while all around them in the corral yard hostlers were peering from places of safe vantage. Pete Clifford was still over in his office doorway. His men were elsewhere, but just as discreetly out of any probable line of fire. That coach-driver who had delivered Whitney was standing in his gauntlets and long coat over beside the shoeing shed, whip lying in the bend of one arm as though it were a rifle, looking almost droll as he remained motionless, watching.

Whitney studied the letter from Durango a long while. This, clearly, was the one communication he had no defense against, and as he read it his face slackened, loosened until he looked beaten, finally. When he handed the letter back, he said, "That could be a damned forgery."

Jameson sighed, put up his sixgun and stepped still closer. "It's no forgery and you know it isn't. Whitney, you're one son of a bitch!"

Whitney took the bait. He twisted slightly on the balls of his feet to swing. He was a powerful bull, but his blow was too long coming. Jameson leaned clear of the swing, then went in, and Pete Clifford over in the doorway said, "You're in over your head, Marshal."

He was right. Jameson was very good at this kind of violence. He'd used it much more often to maintain the peace in Ruby than he'd used his gun. He pawed to clear the way straight at Whitney, shoved the federal officer's upraised arm to one side and fired his right from the shoulder as straight as an arrow. It struck like granite and Whitney staggered.

But the Deputy U.S. Marshal was no novice either, and while Jameson's blow should have drowned him, and in fact it did make his knees wobble, Buck Whitney was ready to fight also. He pedaled backwards to keep clear and raised both massive arms out front to protect himself.

Jameson had met every variety of defense. He knew the key to this one, which happened to be the most common of all defenses. He slid in close, drew Whitney into a crouch, leaned to the right and when Whitney fired his right hand, Jameson was far below it coming up with a stinging left. When Whitney tried desperately to recover balance, to throw up an adequate defense and twist his body, he did it all too late. Jameson's right came upwards on an angle. When it struck jawbone the sound was as sharp as the report of a distant pistol shot.

The watched men groaned. It was difficult not to feel sorry for Marshal Whitney. He dropped his guard, his eyes rolled and both legs turned outward. He fell forward. Jameson stepped to one side, and as the federal officer hit the ground like a half-sack of wet grain Jameson was already turning in the direction of the man who had arrived with Jameson, the stage-driver.

"When are you heading back?" he asked.

The driver was a long moment in answering. His gaze was fixed upon the inert form at Jameson's feet. He swallowed, his prominent Adam's apple bobbled, then he said, "Wasn't figuring on leaving until maybe this evening when I'd rested up a little, Deputy."

Jameson pointed, "Come over here, pick up this asshole and pitch him inside your coach, and turn your rig and haul on out of here and drop him off with Old Man McCallister. And don't stop until you're there. Tell Old Man McCallister this son of a bitch caused all the ruckus up at his property the other night. Understand?"

The driver didn't know McCallister but he came forward to strain under the weight of the battered and unconscious lawman. Pete Clifford also came forward. He started to protest.

"Hey, Lincoln, those horses haven't even been watered!"

Jameson looked around. "Collect your fee from the next chartered coach, Pete. And keep out of this!"

Clifford stood dourly glaring but he made no further attempt to intrude, and as the stage driver was climbing back to his high seat and looked round at Pete, the way-station supervisor simply shrugged.

Lincoln Jameson picked up Marshal Whitney's Colt, dusted it off, and slid it between his belt and his backbone. He straightened his hat and headed towards the café.

Leslie West was standing in the window and when Jameson entered the café he said, "Do you think we can find a place around town for the Hollisters?"

"The girl too?"

He did not respond; he said the Hollisters, which meant both of them. She crossed slowly to the counter and went behind it from habit.

"Coffee, Lincoln?"

"No thanks." He smiled at her. "About going buggy-riding this evening… I'll go make arrangements to rent one of Murray's rigs."

She said, "All right…Lincoln? What we were talking about earlier, before Pete walked in this morning…"

"I figured that's what we could discuss tonight while we are buggy-riding, Leslie. Are you still willing?"

She evidently was because she said, "A woman ready to get married doesn't change her mind between breakfast time and supper-time. How about you, Lincoln? Are you still willing?"

He stood up slowly and leaned across the counter. "Ever since I first stepped into this café years ago."

She started to lean in to meet him in a kiss but boots clumping down outside the café deterred her. As she pulled quickly back she said, "Go talk to Murray, then come back and I'll have your dinner ready."

He straightened up and winked. She winked back, then he turned and walked out.

Joshua Owen is a writer from the Midwest. This is his first western novel.

He can be reached at:

Joshua Owen
P.O. Box 903
Sheboygan, WI 53083